Gestapo
MARS

VICTOR GISCHLER

TITAN BOOKS

Gestapo Mars
Print edition ISBN: 9781783297351
Electronic edition ISBN: 9781783297368

Published by Titan Books
A division of Titan Publishing Group Ltd
144 Southwark Street, London SE1 0UP

First edition: September 2015
2 4 6 8 10 9 7 5 3 1

Visit our website: www.titanbooks.com

A CIP catalogue record for this title is available from the British Library.

Printed and bound in the United States

This book is for Anthony Neil Smith who taught me how to be awful and own it. We don't do safe fiction up in here!

ONE

The first thing I did when they opened the chamber was puke on the guy's shoes.

"Son of a bitch," the guy said, stepping back.

Then I focused on him, all pencil-neck rage and a clipboard and a lab coat. Cryo-lab nerd. A dime a dozen, so I hadn't made an enemy worth sweating. I put my hands on either side of the chamber, tried to pry myself out. No dice. I was weak as a kitten. A hung-over kitten after a triathlon.

"You knew it could happen," another voice said, connected to somebody I couldn't see. "Most of them vomit."

"He moved faster than the others," lab coat said. "I wasn't ready."

"Wheel him to the recovery room," the other voice said. "I'll brief him when he's lucid."

I tried to tell him a steak sandwich and a couple of pilsners would get me lucid in a hurry but the only words to spill out of my mouth were, "sdh glunmg snooj."

"They're always floppy and retarded when they first wake up," lab coat said. "Hard to believe the millions of credit that went into them."

"Just wheel him into the recovery room," the other voice said. "On second thought, get him to wash down first, in case he shits himself, and make sure he's hydrated."

I did shit myself—pissed, too, and fell right into it, the room spinning, air going out of my lungs, legs like noodles. That hadn't happened the other times, and I got worried, even as many soft hands picked me up, hosed me off, and in feminine tones told me it would be okay.

Nurses. I liked nurses way more than I liked lab coats.

Then I was in a set of clean scrubs. Sitting in a chair. My eyes focused a bit at a time.

The recovery room looked just like the interrogation room and the debriefing room. Sometimes it was hard to know if you were coming out or going back in. The guy across from me wore a black suit instead of a lab coat. Ties were back in fashion, thin with a line of red glitter down the middle. He pulled his tie loose, leaned in, and squinted at me.

"You okay?" It was the other voice from before. "Can you keep it together, or you need a little more time?" He reached into his jacket, and my body tried to flinch out of reflex, but it wasn't happening. Too many of my muscles were still asleep. Anyway, he only came out with a pack of cigarettes, filterless Cosmics, and shook one loose and popped it into his mouth, the tip flaring orange as it self-lit.

"Maybe a hypo," he suggested. "Want us to juice you?"

I shook my head. "How long?" I croaked. My voice felt rough. My mouth tasted like some creature had laid eggs in there and then the eggs had hatched and all the baby creatures had taken their first craps on my tongue. The first intelligible words out of my face probably should have been to ask for a glass of water.

The tie and the cigarettes threw me. My muscles were only so much sleepy meat, but the mind was starting to process. Fashions come and go. A while back they created a tobacco additive to neutralize the carcinogenic effects, but then two decades later found the additive caused huge, bleeding hemorrhoids. The fact smoking was okay again meant they'd licked the hemorrhoids, and a chunk of time had passed.

How long?

"You'll need to adjust, naturally," Glitter Tie said. "We'll help you through the process."

I cleared my throat and said very clearly and distinctly, "How? Long?"

"Two hundred and fifty-eight years."

"Sons of... *bitches*."

"Hey, now." Glitter Tie held up his hands, palms out, placating.

"You fucker." I spat the word at him again, strength flowing back into my body, into my voice. "Fucker!"

"I can understand why you might be upset."

"Fuck you straight in your fuck hole," I shouted. It felt good to shout. I was waking up all over. "Every two or three years, and then once for ten years, and then twelve years last time, and then *two hundred and fifty-eight*?"

Training and maintaining a bio-engineered operative was expensive as hell, and the agency didn't want us falling down manholes or choking on chicken bones in between missions. They kept us in stasis, and we were contracted for a certain number of missions. Once we did our tour, they cut us loose.

I reminded Glitter Tie of this.

"But it's sort of tough to hit your quota when you're in stasis for two and a half fucking centuries, motherfucker."

"I know, I know." He flicked the cigarette butt into the corner, then immediately popped another, puffed it to life. "You need to calm down, and I'll explain."

"The fact you're still wearing your head shows that I'm calmer than you deserve." This was bullshit. My legs still felt like rubber bands that had been doing shots of tequila all night, but it felt good to make the threat. Seizing opportunities was a key element in my personality profile.

Glitter Tie ignored the bravado.

"Operatives have changed a lot over the years," he explained. "The game was changing rapidly even as you got shoved back into the deep freeze after your last mission. Intense training and prenatal bio-engineering are only the tip of the iceberg now. Most operatives have extra hardware. Hell, I even have a micro-processor installed in my brain for office functions."

"What's 467 times 231?"

"107,877," he said immediately.

"I'll take your word for it."

"And I'm just a mid-level, government bureaucrat," he said. "The operatives have systems like you wouldn't believe. Built-in weapons. Crazy shit. You know how it is with new tech. Once they get the ball rolling, it's like an avalanche. The agency blinked, and a whole bunch of you old timers were obsolete before you could say Harvey Bangswipe."

"I don't get the reference."

"The point is, you kept getting moved farther and farther down the rotation until it was obvious you just weren't going to be needed again. If it makes you feel any better, it's not personal. A lot of operatives got stuck just like you."

"It doesn't make me feel one iota better," I said, "and as soon as I can make a fist I'm going to beat your face into pudding."

"Don't you want to know why, now, all of a sudden, we've activated you when, as I've just indicated, the agency has a plethora of far superior operatives to choose from?"

"It's the single most pressing question of my existence."

"There's a colony planet out past the rim," Glitter Tie said. "Home of some naturalist-type cultists. They'd spot one of our modern operatives a parsec away, what with all the gadgets and implants. We need a man of raw meat to get in there and infiltrate the place. The exact nature of your mission will be revealed later, when your field handler briefs you."

"What makes you think I'm going to do a damn thing for you cocksuckers when you left me to rot in the deep freeze?"

Glitter Tie sighed, and pinched the bridge of his nose between thumb and forefinger. They teach middle managers that move specifically to deal with dumb shits who can't see the big picture. But for me the big picture was that I'd been screwed, and I was pissed. Anything beyond that was superfluous in my admittedly narrow view of the universe.

"Listen," he said. "We predicted your likely dissatisfaction with the current situation, and we're prepared not only to compensate you in a monetary fashion, but to wave any and all further obligations you have to the agency. You'll be a free man. All set up with the galaxy at your fingertips. No strings."

It was a damn fine offer, especially considering that if the chemical protocols were still in effect, they could basically turn me off with the flick of a switch—and yet I was still pissed. Still baffled and appalled that the universe had rotated around me while I lay there like some kind of half-assed popsicle. I opened my mouth to tell him to grab his ankles and fellate himself.

The explosions in the next room rocked us out of our chairs, sent us sprawling across the floor. The lights flickered, and then went out. The emergency reds came on, bathing us in a dim hellish glow. I blinked and looked over at Glitter Tie, who seemed as betrayed as he was stunned.

"Damn," he said. "I thought we'd have more time."

He took a pistol out of his jacket and shot himself in the head.

I'll admit it. That caught me a little off guard.

TWO

And then the jackbooted thugs stormed the briefing room.

Dressed all in black, knee-high boots, heels clacking on the tile floor. Black cloth caps with silver skull insignias, crossed curved daggers below the skull. They clutched little black automatic pistols in black-gloved fists, a half-dozen of them crowding the tiny briefing room, pointing the pistols, looking for something to shoot at.

The lead thug with captain's insignia on his shoulders put a boot heel on Glitter Tie's chest and shot the corpse three times in the head.

"Traitorous dog!"

"I think he's already dead," I said, struggling back into my chair.

"Now it's official," the captain said.

"Me, next?"

"Of course not." The captain seemed offended by the idea. "We're here to rescue you, Mr. Sloan."

Sloan. Yeah, that was my name. It didn't even occur to me to wonder who I was until the captain said it. Then it was all coming back, faster and faster. The protocols were extremely goal-oriented. Little details like identity always snapped into focus last.

Carter Sloan. Thirty-eight years old (subjective). Six feet tall without shoes, one hundred and seventy-six pounds. Hair: brown. Eyes: brown. Caucasian.

"Come with us, Mr. Sloan. Our orders are to evac you to a safe location, where details of your situation will be revealed."

I stood, legs still wobbly. "I'll come, but don't expect me to set any land speed records."

I followed them through the cryo labs, but my knees gave out in the lobby. A pair of thugs flanked me, hoisting me up under the arms. The toes of my hospital slippers made drag marks in the dust as they dragged me down a long hallway toward the exit.

Dust?

I noticed it now. The outer rooms were a wreck—dust and cobwebs on the light fixtures, tarps thrown over furniture.

"This place was mothballed?"

"The rebels brought this facility back online specifically to resurrect you," the captain said.

"I'm flattered."

We took a service elevator up to the surface. When we came out of the dome that covered the entrance to the agency cryo facility, I gasped. The huge industrial complex surrounding the agency bunker had been flattened, and not recently. Rubble piled up all around us, rusted girders like the ancient bones of some gigantic tortured animal rising into the air. In the hazy distance, the capitol building looked like some hulking titan had taken a bite out of it. The sky was smoky and gray, the sun struggling to shine light through the thick haze.

What the hell has happened?

The captain must have read my mind. "DC was nuked. Along with New York, L.A., Chicago, Houston, Paris, London, Moscow, Cairo—too many to list. Earth was finished fifty years ago. Our capital is Mars now. We hold most of the solar system, although the rebels have bases on a couple of Jupiter's moons. Their big strongholds are out of the system."

"Out of the system?" They'd only begun to colonize out-system when I'd last been sent back into deep freeze.

"Translight tech made a huge leap a hundred years ago," the captain said. "We've got a human presence on nearly four hundred worlds. Earth was on its way to being old news even before the nukes fell. There are still a number of functioning cities, and some good natural resources left to be exploited, but the hub of all empire activity is on Mars now."

The roar of anti-grav generators drowned out my next question as the armored transport touched down forty yards away, kicking up dust and debris. The gangplank slammed down and a dozen armored troopers spilled out and formed a perimeter to cover us as we boarded, but no enemies showed up to laser us into ash.

Once aboard, they strapped me in across from an official-looking guy in a green suit. His tie and shirt were different shades of green, green glitter down the center of the tie. He smiled at me perfunctorily before turning to the captain.

"Captain, make sure the pilot is following the evac plan we discussed," he said.

"Yes, sir." The captain left for the cockpit.

I felt the ship shudder as we lifted off.

"Good to meet you, Mr. Sloan," the man in the green suit said. "I'm Agent Armand with Empire Internal Security."

"Secret police," I said.

Armand smiled vaguely, then shrugged. "It's a paycheck."

"Is this where I find out what's going on, or do we do some more cloak and dagger bullshit first?"

"What did the first man tell you?" Armand asked. "I'll pick it up from there."

I told him, how I'd been selected to infiltrate a naturalist cult, the whole shooting match. I related the conversation word for word. Operatives have good recall. It's part of the job.

"What he told you is essentially true," Armand said.

"Why did he shoot himself?"

"To avoid torture, I'd imagine. As a high-level rebel agent, he likely had valuable information."

"You would have tortured him?"

"Absolutely," Armand said. "I mean, not me personally, but, yes, we would have knocked the shit out of him pretty good."

"What about me?"

"That depends on what the captain tells me," Armand said. "Ah, here he is now. Captain?"

"It went just as planned," the captain told Armand. "The pilot reports that he jammed a rebel distress signal before it left orbit. Under intense interrogation, one of the rebel lab techs gave up an identification code. We used it to transmit a message which was accepted by the rebel base on Europa. In short, the rebels believe their attempt to extract Mr. Sloan has been successful."

"Excellent, Captain." Armand rubbed his hands together, a smile of genuine satisfaction on his ruddy puss. "Please pass along my compliments to all involved."

The captain bowed, clicked his heels and excused himself.

Armand beamed at me. "We're in the perfect position to insert you undercover into the naturalist cult, except now you will act on behalf of the *legitimate* galactic government, instead of for the rebels."

"I don't even know what I'm supposed to do," I said, "for any government."

"All of that will be revealed in due time," Armand assured me. "What the rebel agent told you was true. One of our modern operatives would be detected in an instant. That's why they raided the mothballed facility and brought you out of stasis. Stay patient. We'll fill you in on the details. We'll equip you and support you in every possible way to make sure your mission is a success. All we need to know at this moment, Mr. Sloan, is if you are still ready and willing to serve the Third Reich."

"Of course," I said.

Sieg heil, baby.

THREE

The ship docked with the imperial frigate *Rommel*, which was waiting for us in orbit.

I spent most of the nine-hour trip to Mars in the accelerated gym, working the kinks out of my muscles and getting my reflexes back. An hour at the gun range with slug-throwers and laser weapons confirmed that my hand–eye coordination was in order. I injured three troopers in a hand-to-hand refresher. No problems.

I dressed myself in a new gray suit for my briefing with Armand, a small, tasteful swastika pin on the lapel. Reluctantly, I wore a thin black tie with red glitter down the middle.

When in Rome.

Except Rome had been nuked to shit decades ago.

The door to the formal dining parlor spiraled open, and I entered. Armand sat at the far end of a highly polished wooden table, a crystal goblet at his elbow, a plate of something leafy in front of him. Behind him a huge red banner with a swastika in the middle hung floor to ceiling.

"You're doing well, I take it?" he asked.

"I'm better. The effects of being in deep freeze so long were pretty severe. I don't plan on going back in that long again. Or ever," I growled.

"You might change your mind if you do any traveling. They use cryo-sleep for journeys into deep space," Armand said. "It takes three or four years at maximum translight to reach some of the outer colonies. We've been discovering wormholes, and those take us really far really fast, but there are still sectors of space where a long translight flight is the only option."

I shrugged. Humanity hadn't made it that far out into the galaxy when I was put into stasis. I'd cross that bridge if I ever came to it.

Armand gestured for me to take a seat next to him, and I did. He held up a packet in a thin, hard plastic container and slid it across the table to me. The flap was sealed with hardened red wax, the imperial seal imprinted in it, a complicated combination of the swastika and an eagle clutching swords with stars in the background. It all looked a little too busy to me.

I put a hand on the packet. "What's this?"

"Your brief," Armand said. "Don't open it here. You're scheduled to take a commercial shuttle to St. Armstrong on Luna, where you'll catch a deep-space flight out of the system. The rest comes from higher up the food chain, and is for your eyes only."

"Why can't I take a direct flight from Mars?"

"Anything directly from Mars will be suspicious to the rebels," he explained. "St. Armstrong became an independent city-state just after the big war, and nobody was strong enough to keep it from happening. As it turns out, it's useful to have some neutral ground in the system. The rebels think their agents have you secure. In order to maintain that illusion, we need to ship you out from the moon."

"Right." I stood, tucked the packet under my arm. "Guess I'd better dig into this and orient myself."

"One last word of caution," Armand said. "Using an operative of your type and caliber is more than simply a matter of convenience. Once you're out there, you're on your own. We'll be able to support you at the right time, but for the most part you'll be dependent upon your own cunning and resources. So stay sharp."

"Sharp is my middle name."

I flipped Armand a salute and made my way back to my cabin. The ship would dock at the orbiting terminal around Mars soon, and once there I'd only have twenty-eight minutes to make my connection back to Luna. Not time enough to get a solid fix on the packet's contents, but I opened it anyway to at least get a first impression.

There was a digi-reader loaded with data. Tucked into the inside flap of the packet were three passports. One identified me as Carter Sloan, the other two alternate identities. There was a short, typed note tucked into one of the alternate passports.

```
You will travel in disguise to Luna.
Find your clothing in the closet.
```

I opened the closet and saw the Catholic priest's outfit hanging there, new and perfectly pressed. I put it on, and it fit perfectly. Black pants and shirt, black jacket, even the white collar. At least I didn't have to wear some bullshit glitter tie. Sitting on the floor was a light bag with a change of clothes and various sundries.

There was a slight bump, and the captain announced over the loudspeaker that the *Rommel* had docked. I slung the bag over my shoulder, grabbed the brief packet, and left my cabin. Nobody wished me well or even looked at me as I disembarked. I was the nowhere man, the human nothing. I never existed. Blink and I'm gone.

Such is the life of an undercover operative.

I caught a glimpse of Mars as I passed an observation lounge. Clusters of city lights blinked in sprawling patches, connected by crisscrossing rail lines. A thriving modern world. It would have been nice to visit, but duty called.

I made the PanGalactic Spaceways flight with three minutes to spare and a stewardess with *Heidi* etched on her name tag showed me to my seat. She was blonde and big in that athletic way that made me ache a little. I hadn't been laid in a quarter of a millennium.

I pushed those thoughts away, to be dealt with later.

The digi-reader hummed to life after two

thumbprints, a retinal scan, and voice recognition. It was interactive, which meant I could ask it questions, but that necessitated some privacy. Fortunately, the empire had sprung for a first-class seat, which meant I could fold myself into a privacy bubble. I was sure there was elaborate eavesdropping equipment that could penetrate the casual security any commercial spaceliner could offer, but the digi-reader assured me it would shut down automatically if it detected spying.

There was a list of both rebel and imperial contacts on St. Armstrong and elsewhere, which explained the high security. I literally held the lives of a dozen people in the palm of my hand.

Then I sat back and let the briefing wash over me. The players, the stakes, the details that filled in the gaps. I asked pertinent questions and got good answers. This reader was state of the art.

The new information needed to be sorted and absorbed. I told my brain to sleep, so I could let my subconscious step in. You don't toss and turn when you're an operative like me. You tell your brain to sleep and it happens. You wake up when you tell your brain that it's time. This sort of thing is achieved through advanced bio-engineering, tempered with a good dose of strict mental discipline. The logic centers of the brain could perform miracles of analysis if I stepped back and let my subconscious do the heavy lifting.

Six hours later my eyes popped open with no additional insight that was relevant to the mission. It was apparently as simple and straightforward as it seemed, so there was no good reason to complicate things.

It all boiled down to whether or not I was supposed to kill the girl.

FOUR

She was known as the daughter of the Brass Dragon.

When the Reich originally settled Mars, the planet was divided into three sectors, each ruled by one of the emperor's marshals. The three marshals tamed the new world, reshaped it according to the desires of the emperor. The marshals brooked no impediment to the building of the new Reich home world. The emperor granted them recognition for this accomplishment and dubbed them the Three Dragons. These became hereditary titles, handed down through generations—the Gold Dragon, the Silver Dragon, and the Diamond Dragon.

There was another man without whom the Reich would never have tamed Mars. The head of Reich Gestapo, Joseph Heintz, ordered the deaths of more than a thousand men in a three-year period.

Since that time, labor problems corrected themselves immediately when his name was mentioned. Opposing political factions vanished mysteriously. Joseph Heintz made problems go away in the fastest, most direct possible way. The machinery which built the Reich home world was oiled with the blood he'd spilled. The emperor dubbed Heintz "the Brass Dragon."

A century later, Heintz's descendants would lead a bloody rebellion against the Reich.

"Why am I disguised as a priest?" I asked the digi-reader.

"Most of the major galactic factions respect Vatican Five's diplomatic credentials," the reader said. "As a Jesuit Corps operative, you will likely be allowed more extensive security clearances, and more leeway with local law enforcement."

Jesuit Corps. Vatican secret police. The empire thought of everything, and the Vatican home world was far enough away that nobody would really have time to check me out. As a Jesuit I could claim to be rounding up runaway clergy. Suddenly I knew what was in the packet's other flap.

I opened it and found the little beamer. It wasn't much of a gun, but about the only thing that would fit in the packet. I stashed it in my coat pocket.

The spaceliner was docking with the orbital terminal, and they'd be letting us off soon to catch shuttles to St. Armstrong. I moved to fold up the packet but paused, allowed myself one more look at the image of the girl that came with the dossier.

She was beautiful, of course—twenty-five years old, a vaguely Asian appearance, proof of mixed blood which the Reich used to detest, but which I found exotic and attractive. Hair black and glossy, soft green eyes, and a quirky smile that held some secret. The secret to the universe? The secret to my heart? Who could say? The daughter of somebody important.

The daughter of the Brass Dragon.

Find her. Get her. Save her. Kill her. That simple.

Not simple at all.

I boarded the shuttle to the lunar surface.

The bulky shuttle touched down hard on the starport landing pad at St. Armstrong. The hydraulics kicked in, lowered both the pad and the ship below Luna's surface, docked, and spilled the passengers into the customs area.

I tripped the alarm walking through the security tunnel, and a squad of heavily armored guards with stun-gloves met me on the other side. Beyond them, six more guards looked on, automatic rifles cocked and ready.

Another man stepped forward, no armor but an officer's badge pinned to his lapel.

"I'm sorry, Father, but we'll need to search you."

"It's okay," I said, and I showed the captain the little beamer then dropped it back in my jacket pocket. "I have the appropriate paperwork."

"I'll need to see," the captain said.

I handed over the passport and diplomatic credentials showing that I was a special envoy from

Vatican. The captain looked from the papers to my face and back. "These are registered electronically with St. Armstrong Central?"

"Yes."

The captain eyed my white collar, dark suit, the special silver ring on my right hand.

"Jesuit?"

"Yes."

The captain nodded. "These credentials give you forty-eight hours, Father Argus. You'll need to register your weapon again with central if you take longer."

I nodded, and took my credentials back from the captain. "The gravity seems heavier than I remember."

He raised an eyebrow. "We went to .9 Earth normal about thirty years ago. The tourists were vomiting too much. How long since you've been in system?"

"When I was a kid." I kept forgetting how long I'd been in stasis. Fumbling tidbits of common knowledge would fuck my cover fast.

I slung my bag over my shoulder and started to head for the transport bays.

"Father?"

I glanced at the captain over my shoulder.

"Let's keep it peaceful, okay?" He seemed sincere. "We respect that you want to police your own people, but the tourism board has done a lot to clean up our little moon the last few years. We limit most of the wave junkies and thugs to the basement levels. The prostitution district has been tightly regulated and disease-free since the Social Entertainment Health Act of 2209. Please respect our tranquility."

I shrugged.

"The Lord willing."

I checked into a hotel three levels down.

Once I was in my room, I poured myself a drink from the honor bar and paged through the visitor's information provided by the Luna Board of Tourism. It revealed that St. Armstrong consisted of a large domed park with moon-natural gravity topside, as well as eighty-five levels that went deep below the moon's surface. The bottom five levels were restricted. It didn't say why in the brochures, but I knew it was because the basement levels teemed with St. Armstrong's criminal element. Not even the police went down to the no-go zones.

I sipped my drink. It was only mildly alcoholic. Citrus. Something new or old news? Settlements this close to Earth were always inundated with the latest trends. Only products with staying power made it out to the far frontiers.

Having finished the drink, I sank deep into the easy chair and opened the digi-reader again. I needed to get all I could from the instrument, because sooner or later I'd have to ditch it.

"Suggestions?" I asked the reader. I already had a game plan, but it never hurt to get a second opinion.

"You'll need to make contact with one of the rebel agents in order to secure your out-system passage," it intoned. "You should also make contact with one of the local imperial agents to determine if there is any up-to-date intelligence which might have a bearing on your mission."

"Probably a good idea not to get those two meetings mixed up."

"Such an action would likely endanger the mission and cost you your life," the reader agreed.

"It was a joke, you electronic shit pile."

"I am not programmed for humor."

"Never mind," I said. "I'd already decided on that exact plan anyway. Bring up the list of contacts again. I'll pick out a couple of likely suspects."

In twenty minutes I had my pigeons picked out, but I wouldn't be able to contact either of them until morning. It was getting past dinnertime, so I went to the lobby, asked where I could get a meal without wandering too far. The hotel had a fancy bistro, but I could eat at the bar if I felt like keeping it casual.

I went into the bar, climbed onto a stool. Only the best places and the lousiest places had human bartenders. It was more economical for the in-between joints to use a bar-bot. This place was high end, and the bartender followed his little bowtie over to my stool. I ordered synthetic potato soup and a processed meat sandwich. I ate it and ordered a scotch rocks, nursed that, wondering how I'd waste the evening when the answer presented itself at the next stool.

"Hello," she said.

"Hello back at you."

"This seat taken?"

"It's all yours."

She smiled, put a cigarette in her mouth, and it self-lit on the first puff.

"Buy me a drink."

"Sure."

The bartender seemed to know what she wanted without asking. I had an unlimited imperial expense account, so the whole place could swill champagne for all I cared. I supposed if I started buying luxury yachts somebody might come asking, but I wasn't planning on it.

The girl must have been pretty gung-ho to approach me in the priest getup. I didn't mind gung-ho at all.

She had a big pile of red hair flowing down past her shoulders. Blue eyes, skin so white it looked like she'd maybe never been above ground in her life. Not sickly white. Glowing and milky. You couldn't help but wonder what her red nipples would look like in contrast to all that. She had matching green pastel eye makeup and lipstick. A flimsy dress that went with the color scheme of her makeup, plunging low in the back and showing a lot more skin.

When she shifted on her stool, her impressive breasts moved around freely under the silky material. It was a dizzying effect, and I felt myself getting warm behind the ears.

"What's your name?" she asked.

"Argus," I lied. "You?"

"I'm Cassandra," she said. "Where are you from?"

"Vatican home world."

"That's *so* interesting." She leaned forward as she said it, put a soft hand on my arm. "What's it like?"

"Same as anywhere."

"Wow, that's great. What do you do for a living?"

"I'm a Jesuit priest."

"That's *so* interesting."

"Yeah, it's interesting as hell." I motioned for the bartender to bring two more drinks.

"So what are you doing at this hotel?" I asked.

"Oh, I come here a lot," she said.

"I'll bet you do."

"What are you drinking?" she asked.

"Scotch."

"That's *so* interesting. Men who drink scotch are interesting."

"You seem easily impressed."

"I'm just *really* enjoying talking to you." She'd somehow scooted closer without my noticing, her thigh touching mine.

I eyed her suspiciously for a moment then said, "After I murder everyone in this room, I plan to eat them cannibal style and use their bones to build a scale model of a Viking longboat."

"That's *so* interesting."

"I'll be damned." I turned away, shaking my head. "A fucking FuckBot. For crying out loud. Does the hotel own you?"

She said, "I am the property of Luna Sheraton LLC, a wholly owned subsidiary of—"

"Okay, I got it. Shut up."

It bothered me that I had talked to her for that long, and not realized she was a synthetic. What a putz.

"Are you emitting pheromones?"

Her voice and expression went flat. "This

entertainment model is in full compliance with all local codes governing—"

"Can the lawyer mode," I said. "I'm not making a complaint. I just want to know."

"Yes, I emit pheromones to better enhance—"

"That's enough."

She shut up.

The pheromones would explain it. I was still a little upset my judgment could be clouded so easily, but I had to admit to myself I still wasn't back up to full speed. It would take time.

"Clients charge your service to the room?"

"That is one of several payment options," she said.

"How is it listed on the bill?"

"In-room services."

"Let's go."

A quick ride up the elevator, and a short walk to my room. She was already letting the silky dress drop to the floor as I closed the door behind me. She pushed against me, enormous soft mammaries pressing into my chest as she tilted her head up for a kiss. So I kissed her. Hard.

My erection grew hard, as well, and insistent, and she began to grind against it. One of her hands drifted down to my zipper. She pulled me out and started working me. I gasped, filled my hands with her tits.

She pulled away from me and went to her knees, gently took me into her mouth without using her hands. She bobbed slowly but felt me twitch, knew it wouldn't be long and picked up speed.

I blasted in her mouth, and she swallowed, kept taking it for what felt like forever. I think I blacked out a little because I blinked and found myself flat on the bed. She had already tugged off my pants. I stripped off the rest of my clothing, pushed her back into a nest of pillows. I sucked a nipple, kissed a trail down to her red thatch and began to attack her clit with my tongue.

She squirmed, moaned. Was she faking or was she programmed to enjoy it, and if so, did that make it more or less fake? I didn't care. I was hard again and slammed into her. She threw her legs over my shoulders.

I humped and humped, the two of us groaning and thrashing and grunting and heaving until I came inside her and collapsed.

And then I dozed.

A little while later, I opened my eyes. She was still there, curled up against me, her fingers in my chest hair. But I wasn't thinking of her. I woke up with another girl's face hovering in front of my mind's eye.

The daughter of the Brass Dragon.

Why was the girl with the cultists? The digi-reader didn't know—there were only guesses.

I knew everything I ever would know or *needed* to know about the pretend girl who was lying next to me. Knew she was nothing. An illusion. Yet the very real young lady hundreds of thousands of light years away intrigued me without end, simply because I knew nothing at all about her.

But the pretend lady was here, and her hand was

slowly heading for my groin. She grabbed me at the base, started pumping and I grew hard again, more slowly this time, but without fail. And then her mouth was on me.

I leaned back into the pillows, closed my eyes.

She came off of me with a wet pop, and her tone and expression were flat and businesslike again.

"Your current session ends in two minutes and nine seconds. To extend for another thirty minutes please authorize payment."

A nice trick.

I extended for another thirty minutes... and two more thirty-minute extensions after that. It had, after all, been two-hundred and fifty-eight years.

FIVE

The one thing artificial women have over the real McCoy is that they know when to leave. Cassandra slipped away in the wee hours, likely after I was unresponsive to repeated demands to extend for another thirty minutes. I greeted the morning with room service coffee and showered away the cloying scent of her.

Twenty minutes later, I left the hotel behind me and ventured into the sprawling underground city of St. Armstrong. Immediately, I picked up a tail while passing through a low-class residential section. There was something about the overly methodical way he followed me that screamed *cop!*

I zigged and zagged a few times to keep him honest—nothing too obvious—but I soon decided I needed to use some direct method to make him go away permanently, so I could get on with my business. I paused at the mouth of an alley, looked around like maybe I was lost. I dithered a good ten seconds then turned casually into the alley, making a point not to look back, but I heard his footfalls coming up behind me, plain enough.

I feigned tripping over a piece of garbage and went to one knee, rubbing my ankle like I was injured. The light was just right, and I saw his shadow creeping up on me, then waited until the exact right moment.

I spun, struck hard with a well-placed kick, my heel taking out his knee with a sickening crack. He winced, grunted, and went to the ground, his hand darting into his jacket.

He came out with a huge automatic pistol—a slug-thrower, 12mm by the look of it—but I was already on him, grabbed his wrist, and twisted. He bellowed and his pistol went flying. I punched him hard on the point of his chin, and his eyes rolled up.

The ground shook as two more goons landed on either side of me. I allowed myself a micro-second glance up to see where they'd dropped from, caught sight of the catwalk two stories up. Not only had these other two jokers been tailing me the whole time without my noticing, but they both had to be augmented to make a leap like that and land ready to fight.

I ducked under a high kick from the first one, but the other landed a heavy body blow and I felt a rib crack. *Definitely augmented.*

Instead of sending a spinning kick back at the one who'd tagged me—the obvious move—I dropped and rolled toward the automatic pistol, grabbed it, and came up in a shooter's stance. I squeezed the trigger six times, spraying the two of them with lead, the enormous gun bucking in my hands.

The slugs hit in perfect groupings, three each across their chests. The muted metal *tunks* of armor beneath skin told the story. They flinched, but kept coming for me. These guys had the works. Not just augmentation for speed and strength, but armored skin, too.

I picked one of the goons, aimed at an eye and pulled the trigger. Blood sprayed from the socket, and the back of his head exploded with bone and brain. He came to a screeching halt like somebody had jerked his leash, and then went down.

No time for the other one. He knocked the gun away and wrapped his arms around me, got me in a bear hug. I felt the breath wheeze out of me, little black spots dancing in front of my eyes. It was probably three seconds before the lights went out.

I fumbled in my jacket pocket, my hand closing around the little beamer. I didn't bother to take it out, the angle was awkward anyway. I aimed it best I could, squeezed the trigger. The red beam burned instantly through my jacket pocket and into the guy's hip. At this range it wouldn't matter how he was armored.

He screamed and dropped me.

I crawled away, shaking my head, trying to make the hot buzzing in my ears go away. I blinked my eyes, focused, looked at my attacker.

He lay two feet away, pale and dazed, his leg sliced off at the hip.

"Oh, *Christ.* Oh, man, my leg."

I staggered to him, aimed the beamer. "Forget the leg. You're not going to need it anymore."

The killer inside me knew the job. *No hesitation* was the first thing they programmed into you. The beam sliced across his throat, and the head came off cleanly and rolled away.

I went back to my first attacker, who was trying to crawl away, dragging the leg with the shattered knee.

"Not so fast, sport." I knelt, grabbed him by the lapel, and shoved the beamer in his face. "You're not augmented like the other two. So give."

"I was supposed to brace you for information," he said quickly. "The other two were backup in case it got rough."

"Well, it got rough, and here you are on the ground," I replied. "Who do you work for?"

"Go suck a dick, Nazi faggot."

I whacked the beamer's barrel across his cheek, and that took the sass out of him. I fished around in his pockets until I found his I.D.

Luna Security. Strictly local and very amateur. It sort of made sense. St. Armstrong was always playing the rebels and the empire against one another. It was part of their strategy for maintaining a precarious neutral state.

If these guys had made me as an imperial operative, then that meant Mars had a security leak somewhere. I'd need to relay that bit of information back through channels, at my next opportunity.

Sooner or later these goons would fail to report in, and that would crank up the heat on me. I needed to complete my business and get off Luna fast.

I pointed the beamer at his face.

"You know what happens now, right?"

"Do your worst, you cowardly Gestapo shit."

ZAP.

SIX

My first contact was a priest six levels down who operated a parish kiosk. I figured this was a good risk. If anyone saw me, nobody would think much of one priest visiting another. I kept my eyes peeled and used only busy passageways, moving in and out of the crowd.

Father Aju was an alien, a squat orange creature with rubbery skin and eyes on the end of short stalks that protruded from the head. Aliens were scarce this close to old Earth, but it made sense in a way. Even the least ambitious priest wanted to do more than operate an automated confessional kiosk on Luna, so they dumped the shit job onto the aliens. Typical.

Aju was flat on his back under one of the automated confessionals, wires dangling down on both sides. He worked on the unit with two hands, and occasionally scratched himself with a third.

I stood over him, and cleared my throat.

"Use the other booth, my child," Aju said without looking up. His voice was low, and vibrated roughly. "Satan has rendered this unit out of order."

"I need to speak with you, Father Aju," I said. "I'm Father Argus. I arrived this morning from Vatican Five."

Aju scooted quickly from under the machine, eyes bulging at the ends of his stalks. "Is this a surprise inspection? My prayer log is up to date." His eyes swiveled, and he looked at the broken confessional. "It has only been out of order for two days. I expect to have it operational by tonight."

"I'm from the Jesuit Corps," I said.

If possible, Aju's eyes grew wider still.

"I have done nothing wrong."

"We just need to talk. In private."

His eyes swiveled around again, scanning the chapel like he expected a Jesuit hunter squad to pop out of thin air and slap the cuffs on him. He meekly led me into a cramped little office filled with spare parts for the kiosks. He removed a half-full box of prayer books from the seat across from his desk and motioned that I should be comfortable. We sat.

"I need your help," I said.

"I am ever at the beck and call of the church," Aju said.

"Not the church," I said. "Me—Mars secret police. Activation code 45456."

Without hesitation Aju stood and shoved aside a painting of St. Sebastian getting his ass filled with arrows, revealing the small safe behind. He entered the code I'd just given him and didn't seem surprised at all when the little door popped open with a sucking sound.

"This is the first time I have been activated," Aju said without emotion.

"Must be a thrill for you."

"I don't know," he said. "I don't know what to feel. I am somehow relieved you are not actually with the church."

"Who says I'm not?"

The eyes at the top of the stalks went even wider than I thought possible, as if they might pop like little balloons.

"You are secret police *and* Jesuit Corps?"

"Relax," I said. "The collar is just a cover."

Some of the tension went out of him as he reached into the safe and came out with the decoder relay. He set it on his desk, then hardwire-plugged it into his computer. It was a compact device, but highly sophisticated. It would send and receive coded signals from Mars without the possibility of having them intercepted or traced. It was as secure as anything in the galaxy.

"It's routing through the orbital array," Aju said. "Just another few seconds... Okay, here we go. Identity confirmed, Major Ernst. Top priority, render all assistance. Full clearance. What can I do for you today, Major?"

Major. Last time I'd pretended to be secret police, I was a captain. I hoped the fake promotion represented a real pay raise. A guy can dream.

"I need guidance on a possible enemy contact," I told him. "I have a list of names, but no local knowledge. That's where you come in."

"Infiltration?" he asked.

"Yes."

"What's the end purpose?"

I hesitated.

Aju tried to make a placating gesture, but he was doing it wrong and it ended up looking like he was groping invisible breasts in midair. "I understand this information is likely very sensitive, Major," he said, "but if you tell me what you can, it might help me advise you more precisely."

"I need to contact the resistance, so they can transport me off-world," I said.

He nodded slowly, scratching the little nub that passed for his chin. "Difficult. But doable."

"I have a list of potential candidates. Morris Sherman is senior supervisor of baggage handling at the spaceport. I thought he might be able to sneak me aboard an outbound freighter."

"A reasonable thought," Aju said. "But Sherman was caught in a roundup of… ah… the usual suspects, yesterday morning. There has been a push for added security lately, likely connected to the recent saber rattling in the Coriandon Quadrant."

"Coriandon?" Before I'd been shoved into deep freeze, humanity had indulged a brief war with the warlike but generally inept Coriandons, an alien people that looked like four-foot tall piles of snot and moved around like snails. It seemed ridiculous. So much had happened while I was sleeping.

"Yes, the Coriandons have invaded some of the frontier systems," Aju said, "but this appears to be more than one of their insignificant border raids. Reports are fuzzy, but they appear to be coming across the Demarcation Zone in force, multiple waves of attack corsairs followed by larger support vessels."

Damn. I made a mental note to read up on the Coriandon and intergalactic politics. But that didn't change my current need.

"Do you have any suggestions?"

"Meredith Capulet," Aju said.

"She's not on my list."

"She would not be, sir," Aju said. "She is not an agent of the resistance, but rather a sympathizer. She is the heiress to the Bowel Fragrance line of products."

"The what?" I asked.

"Pills that make a person's bowel movements smell pleasant," Aju explained. "I understand Garden Meadow is quite popular."

"For Christ's sake."

"As one of the idle rich, Miss Capulet has thrown her energy into supporting the resistance via society fundraisers and sponsorship of several resistance-friendly political candidates. Many in her socio-economic circle have turned their backs on her for this, but progressives throughout the system have flocked to her banner... figuratively speaking."

"What draws her to the plight of the resistance?"

"Publicly, she claims sympathy for the oppressed." Aju made that odd alien gesture again which passed for a shrug. "My belief is that she is bored and spoiled and enjoys minor flirtations with danger and controversy."

"And how does that help us?" I asked.

"I believe helping a champion of the resistance..." Aju gestured to me, "...would appeal to her sense of vanity and adventure. She has money and influence and could certainly get you off Luna. As I have stated, however, she is not an agent. We must contrive a way to approach her. The name Eliot Swank is on your list, I would guess."

"Yes." In fact, Swank was labeled dangerous. I'd planned to avoid him.

"Through him, you can approach Capulet," Aju said. "He is well placed with the resistance here on Luna."

"I don't suppose he's an easy man to find."

"Indeed not, especially with the recent crackdown. I suggest you search for him at Bottom Bob's. It is a likely place to start anyway."

"Bottom Bob's?"

"A dank and disreputable saloon on the bottom level," Aju said. "Be warned. Local authorities do not patrol the bottom level."

"Good," I said. "The local authorities and I aren't exactly bosom pals."

SEVEN

The elevators stopped at level eighty. I zig-zagged down rusting metal stairwells to level eighty-four, where there was no longer any power. Chemical lanterns hung at irregular intervals, casting everything in eerie green light.

A seedy man with cheap replacement eyes stumbled at me from a cross-corridor. The red lights in his pupils were startling at first. Probably a war vet gone bad.

"Hey, man," he said in a gravelly voice. "You want blow, smack, harsh, grab, stunk. I can get you anything you want if you got the cred. You want girls?" He glanced at my priest's collar. "Boys?"

"Beat it." Something in my voice made him listen. He turned, walked away fast.

The corridor opened up into a wide chamber, a

kind of makeshift market with people selling meat on a stick over an open flame. A mix of torches and chemical lanterns lit the place. The air circulation system, thankfully, seemed to be one of the few utilities that still functioned down here, so the closely packed, unwashed population produced merely a stench rather than a toxic fume. I passed one woman who looked like a fairy tale witch with oozing sores on her face. She stooped over a huge boiling pot, stirring the contents. Might have been soup. Could have been laundry.

Across the market a flickering blue neon sign buzzed the words BOTTOM BOB'S. I walked through the chaos, dodging people trying to sell me secondhand crap, various narcotics, and merchandise that had to have been stolen—digi-readers still in the plastic, medical devices that gleamed new, and a whole stack of those electronic cats that tell the future if you feed them a credit coin.

Finally reaching the other side, I entered Bottom Bob's saloon and scanned the room.

It was dimly lit. People hunched at tables. The stink of sweat and old beer. The low murmur eased a moment while everyone stopped and gawked at me. All they saw was some dumbass priest. They turned back to their drinks, and the murmur rose again.

I walked up to the bar, and a fat bartender with a five-day beard slouched my way, looked me up and down.

"Yeah?"

"Gin martini, shaken, two olives."

"No."

I blinked. "No? Why no?"

"No vermouth," he said. "And no olives."

"Then I'll have gin on the rocks."

"No."

I glared at him.

He shrugged. "No ice."

"Then pour me whatever you have that passes for gin in a reasonably clean glass," I said.

He thought about that, decided he could pull it off, and walked away. He returned five seconds later with a tumbler half-full of what *looked* like gin, set it in front of me. I pulled out a hundred-credit bill, set it on the counter but kept my hand on it.

"Do you keep the change?"

He raised an eyebrow. "I dunno. Do I?"

"I'm looking for Eliot Swank."

The bartender's upper lip curled like he just sniffed a turd left out in the sun too long. "Oh, yeah? Well, I'm looking for a tall redhead with a third tit on her back for dancing."

"You want the cash or not?"

"Fuck you."

I made the bill vanish back into my pocket.

"Your loss."

"It's half a cred for the drink," he said.

"Or what?" I used the voice again.

He put up his hands and backed away. "Hey, you know what? On the house. Enjoy your drink, motherfucker."

I drank it, but I didn't enjoy it.

Then I leaned against the bar, looked around the saloon. Patrons pretended not to look back at me, but

I could tell. They were curious. A priest getting pushy in Bottom Bob's? It didn't compute.

I gave a wave to the bartender. He came back, gave me the fisheye.

"Now what?"

"Fill it up again."

He looked at me with a question in his eyes as he poured.

"Same deal as last time," I told him. "Jackpot, or I drink your turpentine for free. I just need an introduction."

"Never heard of the guy," the bartender said. "Now why don't you be happy for a free swig and get lost? I'd say nobody wants to hurt a priest, but that just ain't true."

I snarled at him. "Bring it, fatty."

He backed away again, shaking his head, and I saw movement from the corner of my eye.

I tossed down the second helping of paint thinner, turned, and saw the three of them coming slowly, looking unconcerned. Thick, greasy, squat, and low to the ground. Simple, effective bruisers. It wasn't the first time these guys had taken out the trash. Except I wasn't your run of the mill clergy. I'd been programmed with karate, kung fu, and the Martian finger death. I could kill a man eleven different ways with my left hand.

They came in low, going for my center of gravity. The three of them were probably potent in a certain context—a street fight, a saloon brawl—but I was something they'd never seen before. And never would again.

I elected to go with the Martian finger death.

I stuck out each index finger, rigid. The first one tried to wrap me up at the waist, going for a tackle. I sidestepped, thrust the finger into his left eye. It popped and oozed and he fell back screaming, an arc of blood trailing after him.

The other two stood back, then came in again and tried to rain punches. I ducked underneath and moved forward quickly. I headbutted one of the thugs out of the way to give myself room to maneuver, then came up fast on the other, jamming a finger into his Adam's apple. I felt things go crunch in the guy's throat. He staggered away, gasping but not getting air. He looked around with big eyes, like he couldn't believe what was happening to him.

I didn't have time to watch him turn blue. The final guy lunged.

My training kicked in, switching me to karate, and my foot came up fast as the guy barreled at me. A loud smack as my foot caught him across the mouth, and he went to his knees, spitting teeth and blood. I took a step forward to finish him off, but froze when I felt the cold gunmetal under my left ear.

"Not so fast, Father."

It was the bartender's voice. I felt confident I could spin quickly and take the gun out of his hand, but he hadn't fired—which meant he wanted to take me someplace. That was exactly what I had in mind.

"Now what?" I asked.

"See that door over there on the left?"

My eyeballs slid over. "Yeah."

"Walk through it."

I stepped away from him and walked through it without looking back. Closed the door behind me.

The dusty hall was lit by a single chemical lantern. I carefully walked the narrow path between the stacked crates and empty bottles. A guy sat on a stool at the end of the hall—full beard and a clean but old Frontier Corps surplus uniform. He held an old Schmeischester 12mm machine gun in his lap. Outdated military tech, but it could spray a lot of lead fast and chew me up, no problem.

Using his chin he motioned to the door next to him. “In there.”

“Right.” I opened the door and walked through it.

There were a half-dozen guys inside. Five of them spread around the room, dripping weapons, wearing mismatched surplus uniforms. One guy even wore a black beret. The resistance. Just like in the movies. They looked like a group of toughs who had nothing to live for except a cause to die for. Romantic bullshit, but they could still shoot me dead.

The sixth guy wore a medium-cheap gray suit. He sat at a small wooden table, an empty chair across from him. A bottle of booze and two shot glasses sat on the table. He looked at me expectantly.

So I walked over and sat in the empty chair, grabbed the bottle and filled each shot glass, then set the bottle down again. He looked at me. I looked at him. I took the shot glass and offered him a halfhearted salute, then downed the hooch. Bourbon. Better than the gin. He took the other glass, returned the salute with similar enthusiasm, and drank it.

He smacked his lips. “Martian finger death. A

little karate mixed in. What do they teach you priests these days?"

I shrugged. "I work a rough parish."

"So what are we doing here, Father?"

"I'm looking for Swank."

He jerked a thumb at his own chest. "I'm Swank." He was middle-aged, black widow's peak, bags under alert blue eyes.

"I'm not a priest," I said.

"No fucking shit."

"My name is Carter Sloan." The name would either set things into motion, or I had about sixty seconds to live.

Swank rubbed his chin, thinking. Then he turned to the goons spread around the room.

"Okay, everybody out. Go on. Clear out. Corey, you stay."

Corey was sandy-haired, chubby, a bulky automatic hanging from his hip. "You got it, boss."

When the other goons left, Swank nodded at Corey, who took my finger and pricked the end. He took a drop of blood, smeared it on a slide and inserted it into a little reader that beeped two seconds later. Corey squinted at the results.

"DNA match. He's who he says."

Swank blew out a ragged sigh. "Well, well. I knew you were on the watch list but… well, never mind. You've fallen into my lap now, so I guess it's my job to deal with you. Your status is need-to-know, Sloan. You need help getting off Luna, but that's *all* I know. That's all I *want* to know. You get me?"

"I get you, Swank."

"Damn if I know how to go about it, though," he admitted. "We had a guy in baggage at the spaceport, but they put the grab on him. Maybe I can figure a way to—"

"Meredith Capulet," I said.

He narrowed his eyes, letting the name soak in. Now we'd see if Swank was smart, or dumb.

Light dawned and he started nodding. "Yeah. That's not bad. That could work. She could do it better than anyone. She's watched—hell, we're all watched—but her, not so much. She's still an upstanding citizen, more or less."

"That's what I was hoping."

"And you need *me* for an introduction," Swank said.

"Right. I have another passport. I'm about to lose the priest cover."

"Good," Swank said. "Keep the bastards guessing. And you'll need a tuxedo."

"What for?"

Swank grinned. "Because you're going to a party."

EIGHT

I was relieved to find that tuxedos had generally remained simple the last couple of centuries, staying traditional and eschewing the whole glitter thing. Black and white. *If it ain't broke, don't fix it.* The tailor who hastily took my measurements told me I'd missed tails by a decade, but some still wore them as an extravagant affectation.

Then to an elegant ballroom in the city center, a space used for gallery showings, receptions for foreign dignitaries. Tonight it was being used for a black tie fundraiser hosted by Meredith Capulet. Swank had told me he'd be along soon enough to make introductions.

The reception swam in money and importance. Everyone who was anyone—the mayor of Luna, chief of police, council members, galactic delegates, even a few envoys from alien embassies, all in their best finery. Champagne. Caviar. Fat Venusian cigars.

And me.

I glided across the ballroom floor, champagne glass in hand, an expression of wealth and privilege on my face. It was the training, of course—I didn't even have to think about it. Something in my brain said *blend in*, and I responded. Posture, country club manner, entitled demeanor, upper crust voice. I'd been to the best schools. I knew the right people. At least, that was the vibe I was putting out. All fiction. The chameleon gifts of my training and programming.

The crystal chandeliers hovered above us on anti-gravs, making a slow constant circle around the ballroom and creating a shifting kaleidoscope effect, pinpoints of light dancing and washing over the entire affair.

Suddenly Swank was next to me, guiding me through the crowd by the elbow. He looked like a chimp who'd been shoved into his ill-fitting tux, and the bulge under his jacket screamed *gun*. It was so obvious that I started to second-guess his smarts, but there was nothing to be done about it.

"I'm taking you to see Capulet," Swank said into my ear. "Don't say anything obvious—not out in the open like this. It's not the place for it."

"What does she know so far?"

"Enough," Swank said. "It's up to you to charm her the rest of the way. So put on your best manners and get ready."

We made our way through the crowd and found Meredith Capulet holding court in front of an enormous ice sculpture of a Denuvian snow octopus.

Champagne cascaded out of tentacles and splashed into a punchbowl the size of a swimming pool, which surrounded the entire sculpture. A circle of important-looking people crowded close, fawning over her, dutifully laughing at her jokes, and generally basking in her radiance.

I filled my champagne glass and paused to take a look.

Meredith Capulet was a piece of work.

I'd accessed Luna's main data network and had spent a few cred reading the public-domain data available on her. She was sixty-eight years old but looked twenty-two, maybe younger. Every soft square inch of her anatomy defied gravity. The curves of her round breasts peeked out enticingly from the plunging V neck of her sheer gown. The material was impossibly thin and clung to her, revealing everything. The gown was strapless, likely held up by obscenely expensive crawling nanobots which adhered to the skin. It seemed like every turn or shrug should send it falling to the floor, the material pooling like a wisp of cloud around her ankles, but somehow the dress hung on, covering just enough for decency.

Her skin was a glowing white, hair platinum blonde, eyes a piercing green so bright they had to be augmented—maybe even replacements. Tall, plenty of leg. Plenty of everything. Obviously she'd spent millions of cred on rejuvenations, treatments, augmentations, and replacements to accomplish one simple goal. To give every man within a hundred feet of her a boner.

Swank lifted his chin, and caught her attention.

She was laughing lightly at something a fat blue alien was saying, but her eyes slid briefly in our direction and she nodded slightly. The message was clear. Let her extricate herself gracefully from her current conversation, and she would get to us next.

I sipped champagne.

"She's not so bad to look at."

"She'd crush your balls without lifting a finger," Swank said. "She's pure, raw power on this moon. Money. Friends in high places, and her enemies are just as powerful. Gives me the willies just being here. The place is lousy with movers and shakers. If you weren't top priority for the resistance, I wouldn't be showing my face, that's for sure."

"You just make the introduction," I told him. "Let me worry about my balls."

Meredith Capulet excused herself from the group of worshippers, and then she stood before us in all of her breathtaking glory. She smiled at me, and a little jolt of electricity went down my spine straight to my scrotum.

This close I could feel the raw energy of her rolling off in waves. Not just the power and the confidence, but something purely and palpably sexual. It wasn't the same as pheromone implants, although a lot of female agents had used them. This was different. This was all Meredith Capulet. At that moment, if she'd asked for a kidney, I would have cut myself open and handed it over.

Her laser green eyes hit me and she said, "Is this the young man you were telling me about, Eliot?"

"Yes, ma'am," Swank replied. "We appreciate your letting us crash the party."

"Not a problem," she said. "It's my party, after all."

"I'm appreciative that you've taken an interest in my situation." I tried one of my most charming smiles on her, but it was impossible to tell if it made a dent. "Mr. Swank has made you aware of my needs?"

"In broad strokes." She turned to Swank. "Be a darling and check on those arrangements we discussed, will you, Eliot?"

Swank nodded, almost a little bow. "Right away." He excused himself and vanished into the currents of the crowd.

Meredith's attention slid back to me, her eyes roaming, eyelids heavy, lips pursed like she was thinking me over. I could have been a chocolaty dessert she was about to devour, or a bug she might squash at any minute.

"So," she said, "what do we call you?"

"Paul Astor." It was one of the alternate identities the Reich had provided, and the one I thought best suited for a fancy reception. Astor was an industrialist from Io, the moon of Jupiter. Just here hobnobbing with the rest of the swells.

"Paul Astor." She swirled the name in her mouth as if trying to taste it. "I suppose that will do… for now."

"Can I refresh your drink?" I offered.

She shook her head, an impish smile tugging at the corners of her mouth. Glossy red lips. "No time. See that rigid little man coming toward us?"

I followed her gaze.

A hawk-faced man in a formal police uniform was walking unhurriedly but unmistakably straight for us. The partygoers melted out of his way as he came. He was short, but his air of purpose made him seem bigger.

I raised an eyebrow. "A friend of yours?"

"Prefect of police here on Luna," she said. "He'll have bad news."

"Should I be nervous?"

She shook her head. "You're with me, darling. Mommy will keep you safe."

I smiled. "That's a relief."

The prefect arrived, snatched a glass of champagne off a nearby tray, and slurped it, casting an amused grin at Meredith.

"You're looking lovely as always, Madam Capulet."

"To what do we owe the pleasure of your company, Charles?" The smile never left her face, but a tense edge crept into her voice.

"We've arranged a little floor show for your guests," the prefect said. "We'll be arresting somebody here tonight."

"Here?" Meredith let the smile fall. "That's bad form, Charles. Honestly, if you'd wanted to be invited to the party, you could have just said so."

"You're as amusing as always," he said, "but whenever one of these resistance cockroaches crawls out of his hole, we need to take advantage of the opportunity and nab him whenever and wherever we can."

A scream erupted across the room, partygoers suddenly making a wide path as a man ran through the crowd.

"It seems to have started," the prefect said.

Tuxedos and evening dresses scattered as the man turned and ran right toward us. It was Eliot Swank.

The three moon troopers who came after him were less gentle about knocking aside partygoers as they barreled toward their prey. Their power armor hummed with energy, blast shields covering faces, shoulder-mounted Gatling guns spinning 7mm death as their targeting lasers found Swank's back.

He turned abruptly, pulling the bulky pistol from beneath his jacket. Swank managed to squeeze off a single shot, thunder and fire belching from the barrel of his weapon. The round *pinged* harmlessly off the moon trooper's battle armor a split second before the Gatling guns screamed blood murder.

The storm of lead shredded Swank where he stood, his body convulsing, the impact of the rounds lifting him to his toes as he rattled and shook, blood and bits of flesh and tuxedo flying off of him. He fell with a wet slap at Meredith Capulet's feet, a rapidly widening pool of blood spreading out from his body in every direction.

Screams. Gasps. A general feeling that the party was over. People began to file hastily toward the exits.

"If you think I'm paying to have that cleaned," Meredith said to the prefect of police, "you're out of your mind."

The prefect smiled, and grabbed another champagne. "Never fear, madam. This one is on the taxpayers." His attention shifted to me. "I don't believe I know you, sir."

"That's because I haven't told you who I am," I said.

The smile remained on the prefect's face, but strained around the edges. "Indeed," he said. "I'd be ever so grateful if you *would* tell me. It's my business to know who is in my city during such dangerous times. I'm sure you understand."

"Paul Astor," I said. "Visiting from Io."

"I believe the most recent transport vessel from Io arrived early this morning," the prefect said.

"The *Glasgow*," I answered immediately. "Yes, I was on it. Check the computer manifest if you like."

"I most certainly will," the prefect said.

No problem. Mars had hacked into the spaceliner's system and added my name when they concocted the alternate cover stories. If the prefect went as far as interrogating the flight crew, however, that would be a different story.

Meredith lifted her hand toward me, and I took the cue, sticking out an elbow. She wrapped me up and drew me close.

"My escort and I are leaving now," she told the prefect. "Next time I throw a little party, Charles, I would prefer to do it without the gunfire."

"Then I suggest that you be a little more careful about your guest list, madam."

Meredith and I walked away arm in arm, though not too fast. No need to hurry. No need to worry. Within ninety seconds, we were in the elevator and traveling up to the roof, where her chauffer waited with her luxury Pontiac Skymaster. From there we headed through one of the spiraling portals in Luna's dome, on the way to the spaceport.

"Do you have any luggage?" Meredith asked.

"I mean, anything absolutely vital, that you can't live without?"

"No," I said. "I like to travel light."

"Good," she replied. "It might be smart to get off Luna before the prefect starts poking holes in your bullshit cover story."

NINE

Meredith Capulet's sleek luxury space yacht was a silver ninety-foot job, state of the art, with an atomic powered translight drive and bubble windows.

We boarded and she immediately told the ship's computer to power up and make for orbit. I felt the engines hum to life, the vibration coming through my shoes as I stood on the polished hardwood deck.

"Computer," she barked. "Change course to alternate itinerary B, but do *not* log the course change with Luna Central." She looked at me and winked. "The radar buoys will spot us veering from our designated space lane, but we'll have shifted to translight by then."

I smiled at her. "It seems I've put myself into the right hands."

Her smile touched her eyes, which grew heavy and suggestive. "We can talk about that later. Make yourself comfortable, and I'll be back in a moment." She jogged down a narrow corridor to what I guessed was her stateroom aft.

I stood in one of the big bubble windows, watching the Luna city lights twinkle and reflect off the big dome. The vessel swung around, and in less than five seconds it sped toward deep space, the stars floating gently past, then faster as the engines packed on the thrust. A lack of queasy stomach fluttering told me that the ship's artificial gravity had kicked in, stabilizers keeping us steady.

Meredith cleared her throat behind me, and I turned.

If she'd been stunning fully clothed, she was a goddess in her total nudity, white flesh glowing in the faint starlight. My head went a little dizzy.

She stood with hips cocked to one side, head tilted the other way, hands behind her back in a posture of mock coyness, nibbling her lower lip. Her green eyes glowed ever so slightly in the dim light, confirming that they had to be replacements. She shifted, cocking her hips the other way, and her breasts bounced just right, nipples pointing out and hard.

"Come here," she whispered.

I almost launched myself at her, stepping forward way too quickly to maintain any illusion of cool. I got within two feet of her, hands coming up to take her by the hips and pull her into me.

Her hands came out fast from behind her back, and I caught a flash of silver. Suddenly I felt the cold metal of a gun barrel pressed against my forehead.

"Is that the titanium-plated Derringer Excalibur?" I asked.

"Yes," she said. "Forty caliber with explosive tips."

"A bit much."

She grinned. "A girl can never pack too much firepower." In her other hand, she held a little black box with a round hole in the center. She held it out to me. "Put your thumb in there."

"Which one?"

She shrugged. "Dealer's choice."

I put in my right thumb and the hole closed around it. I felt a slight jab as it drew blood. It buzzed for three seconds, and then chimed.

"Carter Sloan," the mechanical voice said. "Identity verified."

If I kept having to prove myself this way, there'd be no blood left in me.

"Well, now that we've settled that," I said, "maybe we can—"

She pushed the gun harder against my head. "Not so fast."

No fair. No fucking fair.

"On your knees."

I went to my knees.

She took small steps toward me until the blond thatch of hair between her legs was even with my nose. She slid the Derringer around until it was pointed in my ear, then a hand on the back of my head, slowly pulling me forward. I could feel the heat radiating off her.

"Come on," she said. "Dive in. You know what to do."

She shoved my head again and my nose bumped

into her clit. I opened my mouth, tongued her slowly. She began to moan and grind against me, still holding the gun against my ear.

After a moment she flung a leg over one of my shoulders, and squeezed my face between muscular thighs. It was difficult getting air, but I'd found the sweet spot and kept licking. She tasted like strawberries, and the thought flashed through my mind that her family empire's line of products had progressed well beyond enhancing the odor of bowel movements.

She screeched like some enraged animal, and then she pulled away. I gasped for breath.

Turning around, Meredith got on her hands and knees, backing her flawless, round ass toward me. She tossed the gun away, and I heard it clatter among the lounge furniture.

"Come on, finish it," she said. "Get inside. Finish it!"

I opened my pants and sprang out. It took only one good thrust and she was wet and hot around me. I grabbed her hips, slammed into her as hard as I could.

"Yeah," she cried out. "Come on. Yeah!" She pounded her fist against the deck with each thrust. Her whole body shuddered when she came, and that triggered me. I thought I might blast her across the cabin.

Then we collapsed and lay in a heap for a few seconds.

At last she said, "We need… we need to continue this in the bedroom." She panted. "These cherry hardwood floors are beautiful, but they're hell on my knees."

* * *

"That was abrupt," I said.

"The first time," Meredith agreed. "The next two times were more leisurely. I like a slow orgasm that starts from a long way off." Her fingers drifted through my chest hair. We lay among the white furs on her large, circular bed, watched the stars blur past out the bubble windows. At some point during our second coupling, I felt the ship lurch into translight as we blasted out of the system.

"I meant our sudden departure from Luna," I said.

"The prefect would have sniffed you out. I've seen that gleam in Charlie's eye before. If we'd stayed, you'd have been arrested." She rolled away from me, propped herself up on one elbow. "Toto."

Toto? I frowned with confusion, then a silver helper-bot floated to within a foot of her.

"Cigarette, Toto," she said.

A small hatch on the bot slid open, and she plucked a cigarette from within. It hovered closer and a flame flickered from a small nozzle. Meredith leaned in, puffed the cigarette to life, and Toto floated away again.

"Luna is neutral ground," I said. "Why's the prefect trying so hard?"

"We're on the brink of war with the Coriandons." She puffed her cigarette, blew a long stream of smoke which was immediately sucked into the ship's air scrubbers. "Luna's standing army doesn't amount to much. The Luna governing council is expected to vote any minute to rush into the loving, protective arms of the Reich." Her lip curled with disdain as she took another puff. "Makes me sick."

"But the Reich would offer protection," I said. "It's Luna's best bet if the Coriandons penetrate this far."

"Luna will never be the same," she said sadly. "It's the freest settlement for five systems. You can think what you want, say what you want—it's wide open. Now it's all changing, right in front of our eyes."

"Social and political freedom doesn't mean very much when you're staring down the barrel of a sonic blaster."

"That's the excuse of every tyrant in the galaxy," Meredith said. "Anyway, Charlie's always been something of a hawk. He's prefect of police for St. Armstrong, but wouldn't mind being chief of police for the whole moon. He thinks rounding up enemies of the Reich will put him in good back on Gestapo Mars. He's probably right."

"You've got a lot of money and influence," I said. "Whatever happens, you'll come out smelling better than a strawberry bowel movement. Why stick your neck out?"

"Because blinding yourself to what's happening around you, with swanky parties and expensive material things, only works the first forty or fifty years," she said. "Even dummies like me catch on after a while. I want to do more. I want to accomplish something more important than making people's shit smell pretty." A mean expression had crept across her face as she talked, something that found its way out from deep inside of her. Her eyes narrowed and slid to me as she took a long, mean drag on her cigarette.

"Enough about me," she said. "Why does the resistance think you're the bee's knees, Carter Sloan?"

"They find me useful."

"So have I," she said, "but I think you know what I'm asking you."

"I think I do," I said, "but that's need to know."

A sly smile nudged the mean away from her face. "You don't think I've earned it?"

I took the cigarette out of her hands and took a puff, mostly to buy a few seconds before answering.

"Let's just say that I'm not exactly sure myself," I admitted. "Anyway, the less you know, the safer you'll be."

The ship shuddered gently and the stars slowed outside the bubble window.

"We've arrived at the wormhole checkpoint," she said. "It's the fastest way to get you where you're going."

"I appreciate your giving me a ride," I told her.

"I'm more than a taxi service," she said. "I've had my lawyers transfer most of my assets out of Luna banks, but when word gets out that I helped you, life might get difficult. So I'll be sticking to you like glue until—"

Something slammed the side of the ship with a loud bang, sending me tumbling from the bed. The room flooded with red emergency lights as the collision alarm sounded.

"What the hell was that?" Meredith was out of bed, reaching for a black leather jumpsuit.

I grabbed my pants. "I need to get to the cockpit."

"Report!" Meredith shouted.

"Starboard engine out," the ship's voice said. "Unidentified craft dropped out of translight and fired. Auto-seals engaging. Life support at sixty-eight percent. Shields inoperable."

I ran barefoot through the ship, exploding into the cockpit, took the pilot's chair, and grabbed the wheel.

"Fire maneuvering thrusters," I told the ship. "Release manual control."

The wheel went slack, I took control and banked sharply. The gunship swung into view on the forward viewports. It wasn't broadcasting any identifier codes, but the light frigate was close enough that we could see the Coriandon markings. How they'd penetrated this far into Reich territory without raising every alarm for twenty systems was anyone's guess.

The ship swung around to present us with a broadside. I spun our ship to give them the smallest silhouette possible, but those fucking aliens had some good gunners, and a barrage of grapeshot shredded our maneuvering thrusters.

"Translated message coming through," the ship said. "Hostile vessel demands that we slow to docking speed."

Damn, we're being boarded.

"Comply."

I ran back through the ship to warn Meredith. Along the way, I heard the metal *tunk* of the docking clamps as the light frigate came alongside. They'd have us any minute now.

I exploded into Meredith's stateroom, lunging for the rest of my tuxedo. The idea of being half-dressed while I was taken prisoner by aliens didn't sit well with me.

"They're boarding us."

"I know." She was slapping a gyro-jet magazine into an enormous assault weapon. With the black jumpsuit, the calf-high action boots, and the weapon, she looked like something she'd probably seen in a cheap adventure movie.

"Put that away," I told her as I put on my shoes. "You can't fight the whole gunship."

"I'm not letting a bunch of alien rapist scum take me alive," she said.

"If you can convince them you're pro-resistance, we might have a chance," I said. "If their war is against the Reich, as opposed to humans in general, we might be able to talk our way out of this."

She reluctantly stowed the gun back in the weapons locker behind her bed. I think she was disappointed at missing a chance to fire the thing.

I finished tying my tie, smoothed the wrinkles from my tuxedo, and walked into the ship's main cabin to await the aliens. There were more grating metallic sounds on the other side of the airlock, thumps as they positioned. They'd probably rush in with a shock squad on the chance they'd encounter resistance. I didn't blame them.

"Stand back," I told Meredith, "and give them room to secure the ship."

Her hand came up suddenly and she grabbed my arm. There was a new anxiety in her eyes, and it struck me as odd to see worry in the woman who'd displayed such confidence before.

"I'm scared," she said. "It's one thing to play revolutionary from the comfort of my own mansion..."

So there it was. The real woman under the

bravado. I nodded, covered her hand with mine.

"We'll keep it diplomatic. Don't give them any reason to shoot."

She nodded back at me, tried to smile, but it died on her face. She was afraid. It was that simple.

There was a sharp, abrupt grinding sound and the door slid open. The Coriandons rushed in and around us, shouting orders to keep our hands where they could see them. It was difficult at first to tell how many of them there were. The Coriandons are oozing, green gelatinous creatures, and they sort of all mashed together as they gang-rushed us from the airlock. Their voices were high-pitched and gurgling. The leader at least had good English and didn't bother with a translation box.

"I am Third Commander Xixleplop," he gurgled. "This ship is now Coriandon property. We control this sector of space. You will submit."

"This is not a Reich ship," I said, chin up, trying not to look worried. "This is Meredith Capulet, a known supporter of the resistance. If you have spies on Luna, they will doubtlessly be able to confirm this. You have no quarrel with us."

A gloppy arm erupted from one of the guards, stretched out suddenly, and hit me hard in the face with a gooey fist. I stumbled back and went down. When I touched my face, it was still sticky. I felt around with my tongue, and was relieved to find I still had all my teeth.

"Your diplomatic patter needs some work," I said.

"All humans will submit," Xixleplop said.

"Regardless of politics. This is the new Coriandon Empire. All species who do not get on board and play ball will be deep-sixed."

"That's good." I stood slowly, keeping my eyes on him. I didn't want another wet whap in the face. "You've even got some of the idioms down."

"Thank you. I studied English as a second language at Rutgers University via StealthBot," Xixleplop said.

StealthBot would explain it. It would give a glob like Xixleplop a chance to remotely operate a human-looking robot, doing so from his home planet. I wondered how many other aliens were sneaking around in robot disguises. Something else to worry about—another time.

"Please," Meredith said. "The resistance wants to overthrow the Reich. We can work together."

"Silence, mouthy woman," Xixleplop replied. "All humans will submit and be shackled in servitude, slaves forever to the mighty Coriandon. I know that probably comes off as a little over the top, but this is policy, direct from the home world."

"You're a gelatinous asshole!" Meredith snapped.

"*Silence*, or we will replace your brain with an obedient robotic processing unit," roared Xixleplop. "It is an expensive and time-consuming process but very, very threatening!"

I opened my mouth to suggest that we all calm down, when suddenly the ship shuddered. We all stumbled, and Meredith grabbed me for support to keep from tumbling across the deck.

The Coriandons jabbered at each other briefly in their gurgle language, and I saw one of the blobs speak into a communication device. As he did, they began to back away hastily toward the airlock.

"What is it?" I asked.

"Several ships just dropped out of translight," Xixleplop said. "The Reich have arrived."

TEN

Xixleplop ordered a single guard to stay behind and watch us while the rest of them made a hasty retreat back to their gunship.

"We must detach immediately, so the ship can maneuver," the third commander shouted. In three seconds flat, they'd oozed back through the airlock, and I felt the vibration through the hull as the light frigate detached itself from Meredith's luxury yacht.

The guard stood, utterly motionless, his sonic rifle leveled at us.

"Now what?" Meredith asked.

"That's one hell of a good question," I said.

The ship rocked again as something exploded brightly outside one of the bubble windows. We all went down hard, and I slid across the hardwood floor and smacked my shoulder against a table leg. I tried to push myself up, the ship still shaking and rattling, and my hand closed over something cold and hard.

I got up on one knee, took aim with Meredith's Derringer Excalibur, and fired twice. The bullets lodged in the blob's goopy midsection. There was a long second before the exploding tips detonated. The Coriandon exploded in a flash, his sticky goo coating every surface in the cabin.

Meredith wiped a dripping wad of green alien glop from her face.

"Gross."

"Come on," I said. "Let's get to the cockpit."

Three more near misses almost knocked us off our feet as we stumbled our way forward. In the cockpit, we dropped into the pilot and copilot seats and strapped in. The engines were out, but I knew we weren't going anywhere anyway. I told the ship to bring up the scanner display and open hailing frequencies.

Our ship began listing slowly to port, nudged from its holding pattern by the near misses outside. The stars slid past slowly in front of us as two Reich zip ships screeched past, coming from behind us, the Swastikas on the rear tail fins clearly visible. The zip ships were two-man jobs about a third of the size of Meredith's yacht, built for fast lethal strikes.

The yacht kept listing, and another vessel drifted into view.

Meredith gasped. "Is that the Coriandon ship?"

"What's left of it," I said.

The Coriandon light frigate spun a lazy circle to nowhere, blast points still glowing where the zip ships had shredded the hull with pulse fire. The glowing remains of what looked like escape pods drifted away from the ruined ship like fiery tears. The Reich wasn't messing around.

I checked the scanner display. In addition to the zip ships, I counted six other Reich vessels. The carrier—from which the zip ships had obviously launched—three frigates, one heavy cruiser, and an enormous War Demon class battle hulk at least a half mile long, two detachable pocket gunships clinging to the sides like lampreys. Not a full fleet, but a potent little battle group, and they were arranging themselves into a holding perimeter, which meant they were expecting more trouble—or maybe just being careful.

The radio chimed, telling me someone in the battle group was responding to the automatic distress call. I told the computer to patch it through.

"Unknown ship, this is Reich frigate *Frankfurt*," the voice crackled in the speakers. "Identify."

"Private vessel registered to Meredith Capulet out of Luna. Thanks for arriving just in the nick of time," I said.

"Do you have enough provisions for forty-eight hours?" he asked. "We are on high alert, and cannot take refugees, but a cleanup trawler will pick you up if you can hang on."

I let time slow in the outside world, turned inward and let my brain work through all the permutations of the situation. Floating in deep space for two days with my thumb up my ass wasn't an acceptable option. I decided a calculated risk was in order.

"Action code 616-A," I told him. "Top priority."

Meredith's head snapped around to look at me. "What's *that* about?"

"It's a long story."

After a nervous pause, the guy came on the other end of the line and said, "Hold please. This has to work up the food chain. Don't budge. There are about a thousand pulse cannons trained on you right now."

"Check."

The silence stretched.

Meredith pierced me with those deep green eyes. "Are you going to explain yourself, mysterious stranger?"

"No."

"I don't think I like you anymore."

"I have that effect on people."

At last, the radio operator came back on.

"A zip ship is coming out with a tow line," he told us. "He'll take you straight to the flagship."

"Well, then." Meredith sighed. "I guess I'd better change. Can't meet the admiral covered in alien slime."

"My men are already working on your ship," Vice Admiral Ashcroft said. "It should be up and running within the hour."

The admiral was a squat, balding little man who fit poorly into a slightly outdated dress uniform with way too much gold piping and a ceremonial saber which clanked and clattered in his wake as we walked down the corridor to the bridge of the battle hulk. He told us he'd been pulled out of retirement when the Coriandons had unexpectedly broken through in a dozen sectors. The Reich, it seemed, had been caught with its pants down, and it was scrambling to catch up.

"That light frigate managed to get off a signal before we pummeled it," the admiral said, "so I don't know what or when something might be dropping on our heads next. We'll render any aid we can, naturally, but as you can see we're neck deep in the shit. I have to get the carrier group off to guard the colonies in this sector. The battle hulk stays here to guard the wormhole. We're spread way too fucking thin, let me tell you."

When I'd sent the top priority action code, they'd checked with Gestapo headquarters back on Mars. All the admiral knew was that he was to help me any way possible, and not ask too many questions. The downside was that my cover was blown. Everyone on board knew there was an undercover Reich agent on the ship, and even though the admiral had ordered everyone to shut up about it, the crew couldn't help but wonder who the spy was, and what he might be up to.

"I suppose we'd have more resources for the war if we weren't constantly putting down resistance-spurred uprisings on distant frontier worlds." The admiral tossed an accusing glance at Meredith. He wasn't stupid—at least not completely. He'd run her name through the computer as soon as the zip ship had taken us in tow and brought us into the hangar bay.

"I'm a law-abiding citizen of Luna," Meredith said flatly. "My political views are not illegal."

"They're not *helpful* either," the admiral replied. "But please don't worry yourself, Miss Capulet. We'll make you as comfortable aboard ship as possible, after Mr. Sloan leaves to complete his mission."

"Ah, yes." Meredith shifted her cold smile to me. "On top of everything else, Carter... *Mister* Sloan intends to steal my ship. Insult to injury."

"I'm *borrowing* it," I insisted. "And if I don't bring it back, it's because I'm dead, so that should give you some satisfaction."

Her smile tightened. "Heaven forbid."

We walked onto the bridge, where a dozen crewmen bent over monitors and coordinated various activities, hopping from station to station. Through the front viewports I could see the frigates forming up to screen the carrier. It looked as if they were preparing to depart. The heavy cruiser was already on its way, its engines firing white-hot as it built up enough momentum to hit translight.

The admiral saw me watching the ships and said, "We're on our own now, but don't worry. The War Demon class battle hulk is the biggest thing this side of a hollowed-out assault asteroid."

"I'm not worried about saving my own hide," I said. "I'm worried about repairs to Miss Capulet's yacht, and getting away in time to complete my mission."

"Long-range scanners don't show anything," the admiral said. "I don't think anything's going to happen very—"

We all winced as a flash of white light flooded the bridge through all of the viewports. The carrier and its escorts had all jumped to translight. That left the system empty save for the battle hulk and the glowing wormhole in the distance.

"They're off," the admiral said. "God speed."

"I know this is a busy time for you, Admiral," Meredith said, "but is there a place I can freshen up?"

Meredith didn't look like she needed freshening at all. She'd changed out of her goo-covered clothes into a form-fitting red jumpsuit, the front unzipped just enough to offer the suggestion her breasts might burst free and make a break for it. But I suppose it had been a long day. She probably wanted some rest.

My tuxedo had been ruined when I'd exploded the Coriandon guard, and I hadn't brought a change of clothes. The admiral's people had kindly provided me with a black jumpsuit. They'd removed the rank insignia, but there was still a modest swastika over the left pocket to remind everyone I was a member of the club.

"I'll have a steward take you to your cabin," the admiral said. "You are both, of course, invited to the admiral's table for dinner tonight. Chef does an exceptional turtle soup, and for dessert—"

A young officer interrupted. "Admiral! I think you'd better look at—"

"At ease, Ensign!" the admiral snapped. "I'm talking to our guests."

"But, sir," the ensign squeaked. "Ships dropping out of translight!"

One of the admiral's eyebrows raised itself into a question mark as he turned toward the junior officer at his scanning station. "Could it be the carrier group returning for some reason?"

The ensign shook his head. "Sir, I think maybe it's—"

"New group of signals at mark point eight off the port side," another officer shouted from a different scanning station.

"I have nine ships at mark point one," a third officer shouted.

"Himmler's nuts!" The admiral rushed to the main scanner display, bent over the viewer to take a look. "I want a full count, and I want it right fucking now!"

A long scary moment passed.

"Forty-five ships inbound," the third officer said. She was a handsome, middle-aged woman with a shocking streak of white through one side of her black hair. "All Coriandon."

ELEVEN

"Sound general quarters!" A second later the red alert klaxon sounded through the ship as the bridge erupted with activity.

"Tell the gunship crews they have ninety seconds to detach," the admiral shouted over the klaxon alarm. "They're sitting ducks if they don't maneuver." He seemed to remember us at the last minute, and pointed at a pair of thrust loungers off to the side. "Strap in. It's about to get bumpy."

Meredith and I threw ourselves into the padded chairs. I quickly scanned the bridge from my new vantage point.

"Trade seats with me," I told Meredith.

"Why?"

"I can see more of the scanners from where you are."

We traded places and buckled the straps across our chests.

I opened my senses and, as always, everything slowed, the training absorbing every particle of information and making a picture out of it. The blips from the multiple scanner screens, the orders barked back and forth between the officers, technical readouts of inbound ships, the bright pinpoints of thrust as those ships grew in the viewports. The training latched onto each puzzle piece, arranged them all into a clear picture of the impending battle.

"Nine more ships just dropped out of translight," the ensign shouted.

"Bastards must've been watching, and waiting for the carrier group to jump to translight," the admiral said. "We must have missed a spy buoy when we swept the area. They've got stones the size of asteroids if they think they can take on a battle hulk, but with over fifty ships, they might just do it."

"Sir, I recommend a fleet-wide distress call," the first officer said. "A few extra ships—"

"Wouldn't get here in time," the admiral said. "Only the carrier group is close enough to respond, and calling them back would leave the colonies exposed—which might be just what they want. We're the whole show, people!"

"Missiles incoming!"

"Count?"

"Two-hundred sixty three," the first officer reported. "They are likely coming in light to test our counter-measures."

"Oblige them," the admiral said. "Give them a

scatter spread, nice wide dispersal."

Four dozen scatter-spheres blasted from the battle hulk and streaked toward the incoming cluster of missiles. Three seconds later they exploded directly in front of the missiles, creating a "buckshot" effect. Every one of the enemy missiles hit one of the flying pieces of debris and detonated harmlessly, still several thousand miles from the battle hulk.

"I want a return spread," the admiral barked. "Target the forward dozen ships."

Four hundred missiles erupted from the battle hulk and hurtled toward the enemy group. A few seconds later, outer space around the enemy ships flashed and twinkled like hundreds of miniature supernovas.

"Their counter-measures destroyed all of our missiles," the third officer announced, still bent over her scanning station. "But ten of the other ships had to join in to catch them all."

"We're still going to have to go dumb," the admiral said. "All gun crews report to stations."

"Gun crews report to stations," the first officer repeated into the ship's intercom. "We're going dumb. Repeat, *we are going dumb*!"

I'd almost forgotten about dumb warfare, a common practice even back in my time. It had been at the height of an old twenty-year war with the Akrohn Empire, and had been invented by the intrepid and headstrong Captain John Luke Pishman.

At the time, Pishman had been patrolling a backwater sector of space in a twenty-five-year-old frigate, recently updated with modern equipment. An Akrohn dreadnaught had dropped out of translight and had immediately opened fire. Pishman's alert crew had launched counter-measures, saving the ship from the surprise attack just in time. They returned fire, only to find that the dreadnaught had equally effective counter-measures. For six days the two ships dueled, floating three hundred thousand miles apart. Each ship deflected the other's missiles, jammed the other's targeting electronics, absorbed the other's laser blasts.

They couldn't lay a finger on each other.

It was all too clear what had happened. As smart bombs and smart weapons got smarter and smarter over the decades, they'd finally reached the point where they totally negated each other.

Once Pishman had made his decision, he didn't hesitate. The older, smaller frigate had just a single advantage over the dreadnaught—it could accelerate much faster. Pishman ordered the frigate to move within point blank range, at which time he launched a dozen freezers full of Swanson frozen turkey dinners out of the forward airlocks.

The freezers had no sophisticated electronics to jam, so the Akrohn sailors could do nothing but watch helplessly with their double-mouths hanging open as the freezers slammed into their engines, utterly destroying them. Pishman then knocked a hole in the dreadnaught's hull with the reclining easy chair from his own cabin. After rendering the Akrohn's laser weapons inert with an EMP, Pishman led the boarding party himself, going through the hole in the dreadnaught's hull to bludgeon the Akrohn sailors to death with cricket bats. (Pishman's crew had won the fleet cricket championship three years running.)

Now Vice Admiral Ashcroft, like so many others before him, followed in Pishman's footsteps, though without the cricket bats.

"Move us in among them," the admiral ordered. "They'll have to risk shooting each other if they want to have at us."

"Another group of inbound missiles," the first officer announced. "They still want to do it the easy way, but our counter-measures took care of them." She peered at her screen, then added, "I see gun ports opening now on the lead ships. I think they're taking the hint."

"Tell the pocket gunships to position themselves aft," the admiral said. "I want them running interference for anything targeting our engines." The battle hulk barreled into the swarm of frigates, and within a second the enemy was all around us. The ship shook with the impact of their guns.

"Open our gun ports," the admiral shouted. "Fire as they bear!"

Six hundred gun ports opened across the hull of the battle hulk. The dumb projectiles were lead spheres about the size of bowling balls, shot with magnetic launchers. It was strictly line of sight, point and shoot. There were also elaborate hydraulic and compressed air systems to fire the guns, in case power to the mag launchers was cut.

The battle hulk fired, lead shot blasting in every direction. An enemy frigate which had moved in close off the port side, attempting to target the bridge, was instantly shredded, the high-speed lead balls ripping through the hull as if it had been made of tissue paper.

Another half dozen ships around it veered off as their hulls were peppered with shot.

The battle hulk rocked and shuddered with impacts from enemy fire.

"Explosive decompression in sections fourteen through twenty-one," the first officer shouted.

"Seal it off," the admiral said. "Deploy the damage control bots."

The battle hulk emerged from the other side of the swarm of frigates, then swung around for another pass, inertia dampers keeping us in our seats.

"How'd we do?" the admiral asked.

"Four enemy ships destroyed," reported the first officer. "Another dozen severely damaged."

"Let's give them another taste."

"They're forming up a little better this time, sir." There was the slightest edge of warning in the first officer's voice.

"Full speed ahead!"

The battle hulk plunged back into the fray. An enemy frigate placed itself directly in our path, and was blasted to pieces. The debris bounced off our hull, shaking us.

The Coriandons concentrated their fire forward on the starboard side, at least a dozen ships firing their broadsides at once. The impacts would have knocked us out of our seats if we hadn't been strapped in. Meredith yelped and grabbed my arm, forgetting her anger for the moment.

Another volley rocked us, and I was thrown against the safety straps so hard I wrenched my neck. The bridge lights dimmed, but came back on immediately.

More impacts shook the battle hulk. There was an explosion on the far side of the bridge and quickly the place filled with smoke. Somebody shouted "medic" as the auto-extinguishers hosed down the flames.

"Vents!" the first officer shouted.

The smoke cleared, and I saw the admiral pick himself up off the deck, rubbing at a bloody gash over his left eye.

"Bastards," he said. "Take us out of here! Position us between the enemy ships and the wormhole. Keep our port side toward the enemy. The starboard side is toast!"

The ship shook with another barrage as we maneuvered away. This time the lights went out and stayed that way, the emergency reds coming on and washing us all in a hellish glow.

"Report!"

"I've already told work crews to re-route power," the first officer said. "Engines are good at ninety percent, but we lost one of the pocket gunships in that last pass. No functioning weaponry on the starboard side. Explosive decompression in almost every section of that half of the ship."

"Make sure everyone gets into a P-suit," the admiral ordered. "What about the enemy?"

"Twenty-two ships remaining. The rest are destroyed or damaged enough to retire."

"Twenty-two. That's too many," the admiral muttered. "Damn it. Just too many."

"They're taking up attack positions," the first officer said.

I unstrapped my harness, then unstrapped

Meredith's, and took her by the hand.

"Come on. We're leaving."

"What!?" It was the closest thing to panic I'd yet heard in her voice.

The admiral noticed us, surprise plain on his face. "Where the hell are you going?"

"The situation has changed, Admiral," I said, "but I still have a mission. I'm going to take Miss Capulet's yacht and try for the wormhole."

"It's suicide," the admiral said flatly. "They'll be on you before you get a hundred yards."

"I'm going to try a hot start," I said. "I think I can make the wormhole."

We met each other's eyes, and in that second both of us knew the score. Under normal circumstances, I would ease the yacht out with maneuvering thrusters and then accelerate once I was clear of the battle hulk. A hot start meant I was going to hit full thrust while still in the hangar bay, blasting out at top speed, more or less destroying the hangar bay in the process.

Telling the admiral I was going to attempt such a maneuver was basically like telling him his ship was doomed anyway, so it didn't matter.

The fact that he didn't stop me meant he knew it, too.

"I'll have the remaining gunship cover you," the admiral said. "Whatever your mission is, I hope it's worth it."

I flipped him a two-finger salute. "Good luck to you, Admiral. And thanks."

He was already barking orders at his crew again as Meredith and I left the bridge at a run. The ship rocked with the next salvo as we sprinted down the main corridor on the port side, the impact knocking us off our feet and sending us skidding across the deck. I recovered first, grabbed Meredith under one arm and hauled her to her feet.

"Keep moving!"

"My knee!" She winced.

"The admiral's faced this side of the ship toward the attack," I said. "If these compartments decompress, they'll seal us off, and then our ride's over real quick."

"Help me," she said. "I can make it, damn it."

I half-dragged her along as she limped and cursed to the hatchway leading down to the hangar bay. The lifts were all offline so we had an awkward climb down the metal ladder. She favored the twisted knee all the way.

There were several huge explosions, and the decompression alarm sounded as we hit the hangar bay deck. I could feel the air being sucked out, and knew we only had a few seconds. I dragged Meredith into the yacht, and she screamed pain all the way, her eyes overflowing fat tears that ran down her cheeks. I slapped the DOOR CLOSED button with my palm, and the airlock sealed behind us.

"I'm sorry," I said. "There wasn't time."

"It's okay." She swallowed a sob, dropped into a lounger and slowly rubbed her knee. "Damn, it hurts. I'm going to need a med patch or something."

"As soon as we're out of here," I promised, "I'll fix you up."

"Go do what you have to do," she said. "I'll strap in here."

I bolted for the cockpit, and strapped myself in as another volley of dumb fire rocked the battle hulk. Debris clanged onto the hangar deck beside the yacht. If more debris fell in front of us and blocked the bay door, we'd be trapped. I told our ship's computer to tell the battle hulk's computer to open the bay door, and for a long, nervous second I thought maybe nobody was left alive to approve clearance.

At last, the bay door began to slide open.

I told the yacht's computer to skip preflight and fire the engines to full power. When the bay door was completely open I hit full thrust as the yacht shot out of the bay, riding a plume of fire.

Instantly we were thick into the center of the battle, parts of glowing Coriandon frigates floating past. In the rearview monitor I caught sight of the battle hulk. The damage to the enormous vessel was almost beyond comprehension. Three enemy ships maneuvered close to concentrate fire on the forward section.

The rearview clouded over with the shadow of an approaching ship, and I was relieved to see it was the surviving pocket gunship, on its way to cover our escape. I pointed the yacht directly at the wormhole and kept to full thrust, redlining the engines and threatening to overheat most of the systems.

The threat scanners blared at me, and I saw a dozen incoming missiles speeding toward us from a pursuing frigate. The yacht wasn't fast enough for evasive action. We had no counter-measures.

This would be messy.

The pocket gunship swerved into the path of the missiles, and the flash on impact was so bright I had to avert my eyes momentarily. When I looked again, the gunship was in two pieces, each spinning at a different rate and in a different direction. The frigate positioned itself to fire again, but it was too late.

We entered the wormhole.

TWELVE

Wormhole travel is always a little disorienting. Time stretched. Space compacted. There was a brief, fuzzy dreamlike feeling as the colors blurred, stars swirling and my body feeling suddenly light, as if the molecules that made up my mass were drifting apart.

Then it was over.

The stars snapped back into focus.

We were on the other side.

Immediately I turned to the scanner. The frigate hadn't followed us—a smart move on his part. Who knows what could have been waiting on the other side? You can't scan one side of a wormhole from the other.

I scrolled through the yacht's repair log, and my heart sank. We'd been lucky to escape the battle hulk and reach the wormhole without being blasted to atoms, but it looked like that was all the luck we were going to get. I set the yacht to autopilot, and went aft to check on Meredith.

She slouched in the lounger, her face an ashen grey.

"We're in the clear for now," I told her.

She nodded, the news sinking in. "That's something at least." She looked down. "My knee is swollen."

I knelt in front of her, and prodded gently. She went stiff, but didn't complain.

"Nothing broken," I said, "but you wrenched it real good."

"There's a med-kit in that compartment overhead," she said. I retrieved the kit and administered a hypo to her thigh. She seemed to melt a little, the pain leaving her like air whooshing out of a balloon, her eyelids going heavy.

"Thanks," she breathed.

I eased her boots off.

"So you've been working for Gestapo Mars." She *tsked*. "I'm a bloody fool. I've been helping the other side the whole time."

"It's not that simple."

"What's your mission? Assassinate some resistance leader?"

"There is no mission anymore," I said.

Some of the alertness came back to her face. "What?"

"The admiral's men repaired the engines, but not the translight drive," I said. "That means a trip that would normally take us about five hours will take three months. Whatever mission I was supposed to accomplish, well, it won't matter by then."

"Good," she said. There wasn't any venom in the comment. More like she was relieved that whatever part she'd played, it had become irrelevant. "I'll never forgive you," she added.

"Nobody's asking."

"You're a bastard." She said it coolly, like it was scientific observation.

I shook my head, suddenly feeling tired. "It doesn't matter. Anyway, we'll have to use your ship's cryo-chambers to go into deep sleep for the rest of the trip."

"No!" Her eyes went wide. Alarmed.

"What's the matter?"

"The yacht is well-stocked," she said. "I'll stay awake. I can catch up on my reading."

"Are you out of your mind? That's three months."

"I won't go into a cryo-chamber," she insisted. "They're little glass coffins. I feel like I'm suffocating whenever I'm in one."

"You'll be asleep," I said. "That's the whole point."

"No," she insisted. "I'm claustrophobic."

I stood and reached out to her. "Can you put any weight on that knee?"

She took my hand, and I helped her up. "It feels a little better."

"Okay... Come on."

I led her slowly down the hall to the life-support room. I hit a button on a wall and a large cryo-chamber folded down like a Murphy bed, a glass dome over a large mattress. I set the controls, made sure the computer was monitoring properly. The dome slid back.

I tapped in the parameters for the cryo-sleep—duration, contingency protocols, etc. The computer would handle everything while we snoozed.

She unzipped her jumpsuit past her navel and shrugged out of it, standing before me completely nude. Again I marveled at her beauty—a perfect body, the best money could buy. She grabbed my arm, not sexually, just to emphasize the pleading look in her eyes.

"Come into the chamber with me," she said. "The computer can compensate for two metabolisms. If you're with me, I won't think about it, about being closed in."

"I thought I was a bastard."

A wan smile. "If it weren't for bastards, I'd have no love life at all."

I nodded and disrobed, and then we both climbed into the cryo-chamber, finding our way into each other's arms as the glass dome closed over us, the circulatory system pumping in extra oxygen, preparing to reduce our brain activity. Soon we'd both be pulled into a deep slumber.

She pulled me on top of her, reaching between us to grab me and guide me in. I glided in and out of her, falling into a slow rhythm. She tossed her head back, eyes closed. Her mouth fell open, a series of little gasps uttered in time with each thrust. Her legs clamped around me, ankles crossing over my ass as she shuddered and came.

I climaxed right behind her, my vision going white, then dark, and then all consciousness left me.

THIRTEEN

The coffee was ready by the time she found me in the galley, rubbing her eyes, stretching and yawning. She'd thrown on a thin, wispy slip which concealed none of the soft curves beneath.

"That was three months?"

"That's the point of the cryo-chambers." I handed her a cup of coffee. "So you don't twiddle your thumbs until you go insane."

She wrinkled her face at me. "I *still* don't like them."

"If we can get the translight fixed, you won't have to go back in for the return trip," I said. "We'll be within communications range of a few different systems in about an hour."

She sipped coffee as she turned, shooting me a glance over her shoulder. "Just enough time to shower and make myself look perfect." I watched her round ass sway as she left the galley and wondered how she could possibly look any more perfect.

I sipped coffee and dwelled on my immediate future. It was likely I didn't have a mission anymore, but I'd been feeling like a man without a country anyway, two and a half centuries removed from a government which had never earned my loyalty, anyhow. Did I even know the Reich anymore?

What did they stand for?

And who was I? Just some obsolete spy. I was a tiny speck of dust in a great big galaxy, and I had no idea what I was about. Maybe I'd disappear, head to the wilds of the frontier, help tame some colony world. Would the Reich look for me if I deserted? Would they even care? Take a man away from everything he's ever known, turn him off for a few lifetimes, then turn him on again. There was nobody alive who'd ever known me. They could turn me off again, and nobody in the whole universe would even blink. I had no purpose, no ideas, nothing going for me except a hot mug of coffee.

At least it was good coffee.

The computer chimed an incoming message just as Meredith came back into the galley. She wore one of those red crisscross suits that women favored if they had the body for it—which she did. Strips of red silk positioned in just the right places to cover the fun bits, but leaving lots of flesh exposed. Her calf-high black boots gleamed.

"Is that an incoming message?" she asked. "Have you made contact?"

"Patch it through to the galley monitor," I told the ship's computer.

A monitor flipped up from the galley counter, and we were looking at the face of a haggard, middle-aged man in a Reich uniform.

"—should not try to approach, orbit, or land on New Elba," he said. "This automated message will repeat in ten seconds." A swastika test pattern filled the screen as Meredith and I looked at each other, both of us frowning.

The message started playing again, and the Reich officer was back.

"I am Major Gunter Haas, currently in charge of the Reich garrison on New Elba," he said. "Elements of the resistance, far stronger and more organized than we suspected, have attacked government strongholds all over the planet. Most of the major cities are in chaos, and the coastal town of South Haven—where the fighting began—is now firmly under resistance control.

"We are abandoning the garrison here in the capital, with the belief that we can be more effective by remaining mobile and connecting with scattered police units which have reaffirmed their loyalty to the Reich. We believe the uprising here was coordinated with resistance uprisings all over the galaxy, but we've lost all communications out of the system and cannot confirm anything. The media has dubbed the past week's reign of terror 'the Red Cleansing,' although most media outlets have gone off the air, some replaced by resistance propaganda squads.

"Hundreds of thousands lie dead in the streets—"

He broke off for a moment, his voice cracking. He regained his composure and continued. "Men, women, children. At first the killings targeted Reich government workers and their families, but there seems to be no pattern now. Armed mobs rule the streets. We've launched a distress buoy, but with communications down we have no idea how long it will take the Reich to respond. If what has happened on New Elba is also happening on other planets, then the Reich might not respond at all.

"We have no way of knowing the resistance's strength. Some of the mobs seem more organized than others, and we suspect some are merely those who are taking advantage of the chaos in order to loot and plunder. To boil it down, the situation is dire and unpredictable, so we are issuing this alert that inbound ships should not try to approach, orbit, or land on New Elba. This automated message will repeat in ten seconds."

I grunted and switched off the monitor.

"The time signature shows that message is six weeks old," I said. "Anything could have happened since then."

Meredith said nothing. She was still staring at the blank monitor, her skin paler even than before.

"That's the work of your resistance," I said. Not an accusation. Just a heavy, cold fact I let drop in front of her with a thud.

"You don't know." Her voice was small, remote. "You don't know anything."

"Don't I?" I slouched against the galley counter. I'd slept for three months, yet suddenly the fatigue was back. I didn't want to argue. "Maybe you're right."

She said nothing, didn't look at me. The conversation she was having with herself was plain on her face.

I pushed away from the counter, made for the exit.

Her head snapped around. "Where are you going?"

"To the cockpit," I said. "I have to scan the surface, find a likely landing spot."

She frowned. "But the message said—"

"We're low on fuel and the translight drive is still busted," I said. "We could do a slow burn to the next habitable planet, and put ourselves back in cryo-sleep, but that would take fourteen months, and we don't know what we might find when we get there."

"But New Elba..." she said. "It's dangerous."

I let a wry smile flicker across my face. "Then you can bring your enormous gyro-jet rifle. In case you want to shoot one of the moons out of the sky."

FOURTEEN

I spent an hour scanning before determining a likely landing spot. The town of Corsica was about an hour from the coast, large enough to have a small spaceport but small enough to be off the beaten path. Calling the control tower got no response, and another hour of monitoring showed no air traffic at all. The place seemed dead, but it was still a good bet for fuel, and my guess was that a good mechanic might be willing to trade his services for a lift off the planet.

After entering the atmosphere I dropped to low altitude fast. Never know who might be looking to take a shot at us, especially since we were landing without clearance. I skimmed the treetops until we hit the airfield, and brought us down between two large hangars.

The view from the port bubble window wasn't

encouraging. Some kind of sub-orbital military transport sat burnt out on the edge of the closest runway. Bullet holes and blast marks pocked the walls of the hangars, and ragged bodies littered the area. There were a number of black Reich uniforms, and a hodgepodge of mismatched olive drab uniforms which were probably members of the resistance who'd gone on to their glorious reward.

Meredith came up behind me, peered through the bubble window.

"It's a mess."

"It's a massacre."

"What now?"

"The computer isn't picking up any transmissions from the control tower," I said. "So maybe the place is deserted. If I can find a tanker truck, I can at least refill the thruster fuel."

"What about the translight drive?"

"That's another story." I shrugged. "Maybe we'll get lucky."

"Get lucky? What the hell does that mean?"

"It means I don't know."

"That's pretty feeble," she said.

"That's what I like about you," I said. "Your wide-eyed optimism."

The hatch opened and the gangplank lowered. We disembarked cautiously, Meredith pivoting constantly with the gyro-jet rifle, ready and willing to blast all assailants into dust. I'd availed myself of her weapons locker. A 12mm pistol hung on my hip, extra magazines clipped to the belt, and there was a small laser pistol in my pocket as a backup.

"Let's try in there first." I pointed at the least damaged hangar.

It was empty. The next one held a sub-orbital shuttle, still in pieces as if it had been abandoned mid-repairs. No sign of people, fuel, or anything useful. Certainly no spare translight drives sitting around waiting to be scavenged.

Back out on the airfield, I took a look around. The passenger terminals were all the way on the other side of the runways and landing pads, but the control tower was closer—fifty yards away across open ground. We stood together in the recessed doorway of a hangar, and I took one more long careful scan of the grounds, trying to see into every shadow.

"Listen to me," I said. "I'm going to break for the tower. You count to five and run after me."

"No."

"I don't want us bunched up in case—what do you mean *no*?"

She looked at me like I was the stupidest man alive. "You want me to run in *these*?"

I looked at her boots. Three-inch heels. "Why the hell would you wear those?"

"They make me taller," she said. "Also they *really* make my calves look great."

"And you think that's important now, of all—your calves do look amazing," I admitted. "But really, didn't you have anything more practical to wear?"

"Excuse me, but I wasn't expecting to spring into action."

"So you have a gyro-jet rifle, but no sensible shoes."

She cleared her throat. "I can see how that might seem inconsistent."

I sighed. "Okay. Then count to five, and just follow as fast as you can."

Before she could reply I dashed for the control tower, zigzagging slightly, but nobody blasted me. I glanced back at Meredith coming at a fast walk, long, confident strides, the *clack* of her high boot heels echoing across the airfield. She looked like the best-armed runway model in the galaxy.

I reached the entrance to the tower, and a few moments later she made it to my position. We entered the control tower quietly. The gyro-jet rifle was long and cumbersome in the tight hallway, so she slung it across her back and pulled a sonic blaster from her belt holster.

We were in some sort of dimly lit reception area—desk, chairs, computer stations, all undisturbed, like the place had simply been shut down for the night, instead of abandoned in the middle of a bloody revolution.

Moving to the elevator, I pressed the call button, but the power was out except for the batteries running the emergency lights. We found the stairs and climbed. On the second floor, we stepped into a hallway. Meredith opened her mouth to say something, then froze. Her eyes slid sideways.

Then I heard it, too.

Somebody was humming.

I motioned toward the corner, and Meredith nodded.

Just as we began to ease around for a look, the sharp sound of shattering glass stopped us in our tracks. A moment later, the humming resumed.

Noiselessly she and I slipped around the corner, Meredith being extra careful to step softly in her ridiculous boots, guns up in two-handed grips and ready to shoot.

It was some sort of lounge area. A fat man in a greasy set of gray workman's coveralls stood in front of an automated vend-o-mat machine. The glass window had been busted out, and his arms were overflowing with packages of cookies, chips, chocolate, and snack pies. The humming became whistling. Satisfied he had all he could carry, he turned toward us and froze, eyes going wide at the gaping barrel of my 12mm.

"Are you going to shoot me?" he rasped.

"That depends," I said. "What's your name?"

"Max," he said. His eyes bounced from my face to the Swastika patch on my jumpsuit and back again. "Are you Reich? Jesus, I sure hope the hell you're a Reich rescue force."

"For the time being, let's just say we're *not* with the resistance," I offered. "Good enough?"

He thought about that for a second then nodded. "Okay."

"Let's have a nice little chat, Max," I said, "and we can talk about not shooting you."

FIFTEEN

We sat around one of the lounge's duramica tables, digging into Max's plunder. He'd decided to share, as a show of gratitude for not shooting him. I drank an orange soda and ate a packet of chicken vindaloo potato chips.

Max recounted his experience since the uprising. He'd been a mechanic at the airport when the shit had hit the fan. At first, Corsica hadn't been touched—the conflict just something troubling on the newsfeeds, most of the violence and conflict happening inland. But soon it became apparent that no place was safe. Residents who could afford it fled to the spaceports, but those were soon overrun and held by the resistance. So people fled to the coast, hopping ships that took them to islands still held by the Reich.

Yet Max, like a bunch of others, couldn't quite

believe what was happening. Surely the local police would get organized and put a stop to things, and if the situation was really that serious, the Reich would step in to restore order.

Right?

Then one day Max was lubing a hovercraft when right before his eyes a firefight broke out between resistance warriors and Reich troops from the garrison. He turned tail and ran all the way to his little prefab dome house three miles from the airport. His first thought was to gather his wife and family and make for the coast, but his wife reported that all the roads were blocked.

They were too late.

So he and his family huddled in their little house, not daring to go outside, covering the windows so no light would escape after dark. They did nothing to draw attention to themselves. They listened as the news reported a rapidly deteriorating situation. Then the news reported nothing at all.

A few days later the radio came back on the air, now under resistance control, the fiery announcer decrying the Reich and proclaiming the glory of the revolution.

And then the food ran out.

Max was forced to venture out lest his family starve. At first he tried the restocking hangar, where ships were resupplied with prepackaged in-flight meals, but the place was a mess, already looted by desperate citizens. If they'd already scavenged as far as the airfield, he figured, then the markets in town were certainly already picked clean.

Then Max remembered the control tower lounge vending machines.

"I don't know how long we can live on Choco-Yahoos and Mongolian BBQ Chips, but food is food," Max said. "Damn, I was really hoping you guys were the point of a Reich rescue force."

"We're not even sure about rescuing ourselves," I told him. "Unless you happen to have an extra translight drive stashed somewhere."

Max's eyes flitted from me to Meredith, then down to the Choco-Yahoo. He took a bite, chewing and not looking at us.

Meredith touched my arm, raised an eyebrow.

I nodded, and turned back to Max.

"Max?"

He looked back up at me. "Yeah?"

"Is there something you want to tell us?"

He shrugged, shifted in his chair, took another bite of the Choco-Yahoo. Swallowed. "I might know where you can lay hands on a translight drive."

Meredith and I both tried talking at once. Where was it? Could he show us?

Max put up his hands, palms out. "Whoa. Hold on. It might not fit your ship, and you'd need a translight-rated mechanic to install it. A lot of ifs pile up with something as complicated as a translight drive."

"You're a mechanic, Max," Meredith said. "You could do it."

Max shook his head. "Sorry, miss. That's about a million ratings above my pay grade."

"You could try," I said. "You have tools here, right?"

He scratched his head. "Well... I'd need the

computers back online. I suppose…" He looked off at some invisible horizon, the wheels turning. "You know, I might not have to install the whole drive. Maybe just cannibalize some of the parts. I could look at your drive, see if the problem's simple enough…" He snapped his attention back to me, eyes focused and alert. "Okay, but you've got to do something for me. Or forget it."

"We didn't shoot you," I reminded him.

"You were never going to shoot me," he said. "You're not those kind of people. I can see that now."

"Okay," I said. "What do you want?"

"My family. You've got to take us off planet. This place is fucked. I don't think anything's going to put it back right again. There's blood in the streets out there, man. It's bad."

"I would be happy to have you aboard my ship, Max," Meredith said. "Of course we'll take you and your family to safety."

"That's not all of it," Max said. "You've got to bring them here. The control tower is a good spot. Defendable. I've thought about it. There are tunnels running to most of the other buildings, and there's a generator in the basement. But you've got to get my family here. You've got weapons. You go get them. Get my family here safe, and I'll do it. I mean, I'll try my best. It's a translight drive, but put a wrench in my hand and we've got a fighting chance."

It sounded like a good way to get killed, but what were the chances of finding a mechanic and a translight drive in the same place again? I stuck out my hand and Max shook it.

"Deal."

SIXTEEN

He drew us a map. Meredith and I checked our weapons and set out.

Max's prefab dome was in a rural neighborhood off the beaten path. Perhaps the word *neighborhood* was being generous. More like a scattering of cheap blue-collar homes at the end of a dirt road.

We tried to keep under cover as much as possible, ducking behind burnt-out automobiles, the edges of buildings, trees. Nobody in sight. Newspapers and fast food wrappers blew across the streets like tumbleweeds. In an hour, we were on a dirt track, crossing open countryside, low hills, and grasslands.

"We're really exposed out here," I said, my eyes constantly scanning for signs of trouble. "If you see anything, go flat in the tall grass. That's about our only chance to keep out of sight." I looked at her and frowned. "I wish you weren't wearing red."

She *tsked*. "First my boots, and now you're complaining about my outfit. I thought you appreciated the way I look."

"You look *too* good, lady," I said. "This is one of those times when blending in is a lot more useful than being the shiniest object at the party."

"I'm learning," she said. "Next time I'm stranded on a planet in the middle of a resistance uprising with a broken translight drive and have set off to rescue a mechanic's family, I'll know how to dress more appropriately."

We climbed the gentle slope to the top of a low hill and looked down a scattering of cheap dome houses. Max told us his dome was number six. The dirt trail led straight through the little village, but we were too far away to make out numbers. There weren't any personal transports in front of any of the domes—all the neighbors had cleared out weeks ago. He'd broken into all of their domes, looking for food without finding much.

I was about to suggest that we trudge down the hill and find number six when I saw the group of them come circling around one of the domes on the far side of the village. I grabbed Meredith by the wrist and pulled her down into the long grass, putting us flat on our bellies.

"What is it?" she whispered.

"Over there," I hissed. "Look."

Five of them in raggedy fatigues and floppy bush hats. At least three had submachine guns slung on their shoulders, and the other two had pistols hung from their belts. One of them kicked in the door to the nearest dome, entered, and came out again five seconds later, shaking his head.

"They're scavenging," I said.

They went to the next dome, kicked in the door, repeated the procedure.

"Max's family," hissed Meredith. "They'll find them."

"I know."

Running down there and gunning it out with them was a non-starter, but we had to come up with something, and fast. They were already moving to the next dome. Sooner or later they'd come to number six.

"How are you with that gyro-jet rifle?"

She frowned. "I've never fired it."

"Hand it over."

I checked the magazine and flipped up the digi-scope, sighted down the barrel toward the group, flicking the zoom and bringing them up close. I could see them in detail now. Greasy unshaven faces—hard, gaunt-looking men. They were the sort who would slit your throat for a stack of pancakes, and then light your dead body on fire for the butter and syrup.

The Heckler & Remington nine-gauge gyro-jet rifle was, in fact, just about the perfect weapon for this situation. For in-close work it's no good—the gyro-jet shells need at least twenty feet to work up a good head of steam. But for long range, with an expensive and accurate scope—which this was—a sniper could do a lot worse than hunker down hidden in tall grass at the top of a hill.

The explosive tips of each gyro-jet shell could

punch through all but the best and thickest armor. The more I thought about it, the more I couldn't wait to squeeze the trigger.

So I stopped waiting. The rifle bucked in my hands, the shell speeding toward the guy I'd pegged as the leader. His head exploded in a spray of red mist before they'd even heard the shot.

I watched the mayhem in the scope, the others darting in different directions, trying to figure out where the shot had come from so they'd know where to hide. I shot again just as a burly fellow dove behind a row of trashcans, caught him in the shoulder. I saw the arm fly up and spin away, still clutching a pistol as the rest of his body landed hard behind the cans. He'd bleed out back there so I forgot about him, swinging the rifle back toward the others.

They wised up, figured the general direction the shots had come from, and were sprinting the opposite way—away from me and the dome village. I took aim on the center guy's back, sticking the crosshairs right between his shoulder blades, but I didn't shoot. Not yet. I was playing now, seeing what I could do.

Let him run.

Another ten yards.

Twenty... Thirty.

They were reaching the limits of the rifle now. A bead of sweat rolled down my nose as I held the rifle perfectly still, gaze unwavering. They were so far away, the shot was all but impossible.

I fired.

It was too far. I missed the center of his back.

And hit him just below the left knee.

He flipped end over end, the left calf flying away in a spray of blood. His pals didn't even slow down, kept running until they were nothing more than terrified dots on the horizon.

I rose to one knee, scanned the area with the rifle's digi-scope. All clear. I stood, handed the rifle to Meredith standing next to me, turned to look at her when she didn't take it.

She took a step back, and looked at me like I was a stranger, like I was some evil thing that had slithered out of the sewer. Her face so pale.

I realized I'd been smiling. Pleased with myself.

I let the smile drop.

"What did you think this gun did?" I asked her. "Who did you think I was? This isn't your black-tie revolution, rich girl. This is the real thing. Everyone out here is playing for keeps." I was starting to get irritated. "Max is cowering back at the airfield because he's worried every day that his wife will be raped and his kids sold into slavery by those guys I just blew apart. Wrap your head around it." I held out the rifle again. "Now take your goddamned gun."

She took it from me slowly, not able to meet my eyes.

We turned and walked down the hill. I felt her gaze on my back. She hadn't deserved that. She wasn't equipped for any of this, didn't know she'd thrown in with a killer.

I'd been so damn proud of myself, thought I was such a big man cutting down those hoods from my hiding place in the grass. Then to turn and see the stricken look on her face, like some betrayal. But all she'd really seen was the truth. The truth about me, that I was a killer, that I was some*thing* manufactured in a lab to serve the Reich. To murder at the pleasure of all the fat-cat thugs back on Gestapo Mars. She saw the truth of me and in that instant I'd hated her for it.

There was no place I could go in the entire galaxy to escape who I was, *what* I was. I could go back into cryo for a thousand years, and when they thawed me out again, I'd still be staring a great big fake in the face every morning when I shaved.

I shook it off—plucked the bad feelings out of my brain the way you'd pick a stray hair out of a cup of potato salad, and flicked it away. The training again, the strict mental conditioning. The Reich couldn't afford to have an agent go down because of self-esteem problems.

All business again. Game face.

I drew my pistol as we passed the first dome, and started counting off the numbers, paused when we found number six. I knocked on the front door and stood to the side.

"You might want to stand back."

"Why?" asked Meredith.

A trio of bangs thundered on the other side as three holes appeared in the door. Meredith screamed and dove into a bed of marigolds.

"That's why," I said.

I raised my voice. "Mrs. Jablonski?" I said. "Your husband Max sent us. Please don't shoot."

The muffled voice on the other side of the door said, "You go to hell, you lying fucker! I got a thermal grenade in here and I'll flash-fry your ass clear to hell!"

"Sylvia, isn't it? Sylvia, Max is waiting for you and the kids in the control tower," I shouted. "We've got a ship, and we're trying to get us all off planet."

A pause.

"How do I know I can trust you?" she asked.

I sighed, rolled my eyes. Max had foreseen this. "He told me about your birthmark," I shouted. "On your left butt cheek, in the shape of a spider."

Meredith smirked at me from the marigolds.

Another pause, longer this time.

A latch clicked, and then slowly the front door creaked open. A sturdy woman came out, black hair with flecks of gray. From somewhere, my brain found the words *frontier stock*. Two children stood behind her—boys, one seven or eight years old, the other maybe eleven, both with wide, haunted eyes. I didn't even want to guess what their lives had been like these last few weeks.

"Come with us, ma'am," I said. "We'll keep you safe."

She studied my face for a long moment then nodded curtly. "Give me five minutes," she said. "I'll pack a few things."

SEVENTEEN

Max and I pushed the big handcart along the dim tunnel. So far the spaceport's emergency lights had held up. I planned to be long gone before they faded.

"Flip on that radio again," I said.

Max frowned. "It's just the same shit, over and over."

"I'm new on this planet, remember?"

"Okay, you're the boss." Max snapped on the little radio hanging from the side of the cart.

"—to this frequency for Revolutionary Radio," a smooth voice said through the static. "We have burnt the world of the Reich to the ground, and from the ashes we will rebuild a *better* society, a *just* society, but we can't do it without you, friends. Even now, pockets of Reich resistance threaten our new world order. If you see something, say something. Tell one of our roaming justice squads if there are still Reich scum hiding in your neighborhood."

Max shook his head. "The guys killing and raping across the countryside are called *justice squads* now," he said. "I mean, what the fuck? The Reich wasn't perfect, but it was good enough. Sure they controlled what was in the newsfeeds, and regulated the information we got, but that was to maintain a stable society, right? If riots in the streets and mass starvation are their idea of justice, they can keep it."

I tuned him out so I could focus on the radio.

"For our friends under siege in North Hamburg, hang tough," the voice said. "Help is on the way. Everywhere the Nazi scum attack, our righteous brethren turn them back. We have the power of justice on our side. But, friends, I need to make you aware of an even greater threat. Something that could threaten all of our achievements so far. There are those even worse than the Reich—extremists so vile they would squash even what little freedom we had before, in their obsessive quest for total purity."

My ears perked up, and I saw Max was listening closely, too.

This was new territory for the radio voice.

"My friends, I speak of the Dragon Nazis, those elitist, fascist, naturalist assholes safely ensconced on their fortified island. They think they are safe, but our people know their movements and their plans. Oh yes, friends, we have our ways. Tune in tonight for the evening broadcast, and we shall reveal even more. In the meantime, stay strong."

I looked at Max. "Dragon Nazis?"

He shrugged. "Never heard of 'em."

I had my suspicions, but said nothing.

"How much farther?" I asked.

"Your lady friend parked her ship near the commercial hangars," Max explained. "We're going to the government hangars. This tunnel is a straight shot. Don't have to expose ourselves and get ass-raped by a fucking justice squad."

"They've been doing a lot of that, have they?"

"Oh, hell, I don't know, but they sure as hell ain't worried about justice. Just gangs of dumb fucks, looting and killing. I saw a bunch of 'em take a woman out of her vehicle and shoot her in the side of the head just because she had a government tag. Probably worked at a toll booth or some shit, and they killed her for it."

We reached the double doors to the government hangar. Normally they'd split open for us automatically, but not so much with the power out. Max removed a maintenance panel near the doors and started turning an iron wheel to crank them open manually. The wheel must not have been used in a while, because it refused to move at first. Max's muscles bunched beneath his coveralls as he wrenched the wheel loose, the door opening a few inches at a time. He was covered with sweat by the time he was finished.

We pushed the cart through and the area on the other side opened up into a large hangar. The lumpy starship sitting in front of us had been there since the planetary uprising. It was on a huge lift which had been lowered to an underground maintenance chamber. Most likely that was why it hadn't been looted, like everything else.

We might have just taken this ship, since the translight drive worked, but the ship was in for repairs because the life support was shot. And anyway, it was only a two-seater. The little craft was a postal delivery ship which served a six-planet route in the cluster.

Max was pretty sure some of the parts could be used to repair Meredith's yacht. He entered the code on the keypad near the ship's main hatch. There was a muffled clunk as the power system came online. The interior lights flickered in the portholes, and the hatch slid open.

Inside, he headed aft to find the parts while I scavenged the rest of the ship for anything useful. There was a small closet with a pressure suit and a box of tools similar to ones Max already had. No food or weapons.

Max returned with some unrecognizable parts that he said would make Meredith's translight drive work, so I helped him load them onto the cart and we headed back to Meredith's yacht.

"What are we looking at, time-wise?" I asked him.

Max squinted at our haul, rubbed his chin. "A few hours to install the new parts and run a diagnostic through the ship's computers, but we can't jump with cold coils. They'll have to charge overnight. First thing in the morning we'll be good to go."

"But where? That's the real question. With revolution sprouting in every system, we need to know which planets are safe, and which aren't."

"Revolution might be a moot point," Max said. "If

what you said about the Coriandon is true, all of human space might be overrun with big snotty blobs by now."

"Well, our first priority is to get off *this* planet," I said. "Once we're in open space we can try to pick up some signal, maybe catch up on current events."

That night, I lay next to Meredith trying not to belch up my vending machine dinner of Cayenne Crunches, Marshmallow Fluffs, and cream soda. There'd been a small store of food aboard Meredith's yacht, but she'd given it to Max and his family, saying that the children at least needed to have a proper meal.

We curled together in the stateroom of her yacht. Max and his family had spread out through the rest of the ship. It was a bit crowded, but Meredith's yacht had become a lifeboat now. The impromptu rescue mission made me feel better in all the obvious ways. Support the Reich or support the rebels, either way, Max and his family didn't deserve to have their simple lives knocked into the toilet and flushed. I wasn't an operative on a mission, not any longer. I was just a man doing the right thing for people that needed help.

Yet my thoughts drifted ever back to the daughter of the Brass Dragon. A mysterious creature with eyes like deep wells, and no way to know what—if anything—was at the bottom. She was a mystery that would never be solved.

I was relieved.

A little sad, too.

And that was funny, and made me smile because I was stupid.

Meredith nuzzled closer, her sigh a light and airy thing, a noise a drunk fairy might make, contented without really knowing or caring why. I wanted to be there with her. If the Coriandon had broken through and overthrown the Reich, then I was free. What that meant seemed as mysterious and as far away as the daughter of the Brass Dragon.

The galaxy still seemed unreal to me, something thrown together by a confidence trickster while I was looking the other way, a matte painting tossed up to make me think I was where I was supposed to be. Except the man behind the curtain—the one pulling the strings—had been replaced by a chimp pumped full of meth. Planets and stars flew every which way, bumping or not, and there seemed to be little rhyme or reason.

Order. Chaos. A grilled cheese sandwich.

None of it mattered.

Except it did because it *had* to. How could anyone live if it didn't matter? Why even get up in the morning? Maybe if I—

I sat up in bed, Meredith rolling off me and starting awake.

"What is it?" Voice foggy with sleep.

"Somebody's out there," I whispered.

Through the big bubble window I saw a half dozen flashlight beams playing in the darkness between hangars.

"Who is it?" she asked. "Have they seen us?" An edge of panic in her voice now. "What do we do?"

"Open your weapons locker." I pulled on my pants and shoes.

She punched in the code, and the hatch slide aside. I took the sniper rifle and slung it across my back. Two big pistols and a belt with extra magazines, 12mm with exploding tips. There was a little shredder with a barrel clip, probably about ten thousand rounds. I took it, cocked it.

"I've got to go out there."

"No," she said. "We're locked in. Stay. It'll be okay."

"No," I said. "It won't. Because we don't know how many of them are out there or what they have. If they have a shoulder-launched missile or a mounted laser, then this ship isn't getting far. It'll be a sitting duck as soon as it lifts off."

"But—"

"You've got to get dressed *now*, and help Max with preflight."

She looked at me and I looked at her and the whole story was right there in the silence between us. And then I told her the lie we both knew was coming.

"I'll be right back."

One of her hands went behind my head, pulled me close, and she kissed me hard. We kept it that way for what seemed like a long time, but really it was only a second or two.

I pulled away. "Help Max." Then I was vaguely aware of Meredith reaching for her clothes as I left the main cabin behind and padded through to the lounge. I stepped over Max's kids, Seth and Gerald, who'd made a nest of blankets and comforters. Max and his wife slept on the acceleration couch, which folded out into a double bed.

I put my hand over his mouth, and his eyes popped open.

"It's me," I whispered. "You need to listen to me and do everything I say, okay?"

He nodded, and I took the hand away.

"We can't wait," I whispered. "There are people outside, and we all know it's not a rescue party. It's people who are going to want to kill us and take what we have. Maybe that means raping the women. I don't know about the children. I'm going outside to kill them. When I go out the rear hatch, you close it again. Just pray the coils have charged enough. Give me sixty seconds to draw them away, then fire the engines.

"Nod your head if you understand."

Max nodded.

"Follow me."

We stepped back over the kids and moved quickly aft. I opened the hatch and stepped out. The night was cooler than I thought it would be. I should've grabbed a shirt. Too late now.

"Okay," I told Max. "Close it."

"How long do I wait?" Max whispered. "For you to come back, I mean."

"Don't wait."

A pause. He looked back into the ship, and I knew he was thinking about his wife and children. I'd laid it on thick just for this moment, about what could happen if they caught us.

He turned back and offered his hand.

"Good luck."

I shook it. "And you."

EIGHTEEN

I was already turning away when I heard the hatch click shut again. No time to dwell on what I was leaving behind. I moved sideways fast, targeted the flashlight beams, and fired a short burst from the shredder.

It blasted about five hundred rounds a second, and a "round" was a little razor-sharp needle about a quarter-inch long. Not much use against a trooper in full power armor, but clothing and flesh might as well be wet tissue.

Short bursts at the beams followed by screams. I knew they'd see the muzzle flash, so I made the bursts quick and kept moving, leading them away from Meredith and the others. Some of them returned fire, shooting at the spot where they'd last seen me. It sounded like small arms mostly, mid-caliber pistols, but they still could have something big in reserve.

They'd wised up and put out the flashlights. There was a lull in the gunfire and I closed my eyes, opening my other senses to the night. I heard their steps, movement, crouching for cover, shifting in the darkness. Maybe twenty of them. It was a guess, but a calculated one. I gauged the distance and gave them five more seconds to feel brave enough to break cover and come looking for me.

Then I cut loose with the shredder.

I hosed down the area where I thought most of them were gathered. A storm of deadly pinpricks sprayed the intruders and the hangar behind them, sparking and *tinging* off metal. The men who immediately dove flat to the ground saved themselves, for the most part. Any who turned and ran took it in the back, going down screaming and bloody.

It took a full ten seconds to empty the weapon. I'd stood in one place too long. They returned fire, still not seeing me in the darkness but making a pretty good guess. Bullets whizzed past, inches away. I tossed aside the empty shredder, turned, and ran for the control tower, unslinging the rifle. I stopped every three seconds and took a knee to fire back at them, not hitting anything, but I still wanted them following the muzzle flash.

About the time I reached the tower, the engines of Meredith's ship fired. It rose into the air, turning slowly and angling to launch for orbit. The engines flared bright and the ship shot away. In the glow of the engine thrust, I momentarily saw the scavengers coming across the clearing.

There were still a dozen of them, and they were

a lot closer than I'd thought. I dropped the rifle and pulled the pistols, blasting off a half dozen shots to slow them up, then entering the tower. There was no more time for hesitation. I took the long service tunnel Max and I had taken to the underground maintenance hangar. I'd asked him to give me the code that let me into the postal ship. Some instinct had told me I might need a plan B.

Unfortunately, my instinct had been right on the money.

I keyed in the code, entered the little spacecraft, and locked the hatch behind me.

"Lights," I said, then, "Computer, do you have a quick-start option?"

The lights flickered on in the main cabin. I felt the deck hum beneath my feet as systems came online.

"Quick-start option available," the computer in dulcet tones said. "However, for safety concerns and optimum performance, the manufacturers recommend a full and complete startup pro—"

"Shove it up your ass and start the ship."

"I am a Hamilton-Douglas K-class ship's systems computer. It is anatomically impossible for me to—"

"Just start the fucking ship!"

The computer blooped and beeped, lights blinking around me. I grabbed the pressure suit from the locker and checked the air gauge. Half a tank. It would have to be enough. I put it on.

Then I headed for the cockpit.

"Quick-start sequence halted." The computer voice almost seemed smug about it.

"What the hell?"

"The maintenance log indicates that repairs to the life support system have yet to be completed."

"Override."

"The oxygen currently contained within the spacecraft is not sufficient to reach any destination."

"I appreciate your concern, but just do like I tell you, you stupid machine."

A pause.

"I am authorized to intervene if pilot error seems inevitable." The computer sounded eager, like maybe it had been waiting for this chance all its life.

"Look, I'm wearing a pressure suit, okay?"

"The oxygen capacity in your standard-issue pressure suit is insufficient to reach any destination currently in my data bank."

"I'm not interested in a destination," I shouted. "I just want to get the fuck out of here!"

Another pause.

"Please provide an explanation."

"What?"

"All Hamilton-Douglas K-class ships' systems computers are equipped with state-of-the-art problem-solving and decision-making artificial intelligence software. I must determine if your intended use of this government postal ship is in keeping with—"

"The government who owns you has fallen," I said. "There are men chasing me who want to kill me. I'm trying to escape, and you're wasting time."

"Your life is at stake?"

"That's what I just said."

Another brief pause.

"Preservation of human life falls within

acceptable parameters." I swear the fucking thing sounded disappointed.

Strapping myself into the pilot's seat, I sealed on my helmet. "Open the hangar doors overhead," I told the computer.

"As the result of the starport electrical outage, there is insufficient power to open the hangar doors and operate the aircraft elevator," the computer said cheerfully.

"Well, you don't have to sound so glad about it."

"I am incapable of gladness or any other emotion."

I glanced out the cockpit window. No sign of the scavengers. If they were still coming, then they were being careful about it. I still felt pretty urgent about hauling my ass out of there.

"Computer, are the hangar doors armed with explosive bolts to open them in an emergency?"

Something that sounded like a sigh.

"Yes."

"Did you just sigh?"

"No."

"I heard something that sounded like a sigh," I insisted.

"Clearing ship's vents is routine for cabin pressurization."

"Just blow the fucking explosive bolts."

The ship shook with a sharp crack as the bolts blew overhead.

"Are we clear or not?"

"Clear," the computer confirmed.

I slammed the throttle forward and the ship shot up straight into the air, pressing me down hard in my seat. For the briefest second, I thought the computer might be lying, that the ship would smash against the still-closed hangar doors, and I would be vaporized instantly in fiery death.

I wasn't.

The ship blasted clear of the hangar, g-forces still pinning me down until the acceleration dampers kicked in. I leaned forward and flipped the switch for the after-camera, and an image of the spaceport below flickered onto the monitor, growing smaller by the second.

I scanned the area ahead, caught a blip vanishing from orbit, and hoped it was Meredith's ship jumping to translight. There wasn't anything more I could do for her or Max and his family, at least not at the moment. I had to think of my own safety, and the pressure suit had a limited amount of air. I had to do something.

The only thing I could think of was to call up a map of the planet. Maybe I could find an out-of-the-way place to land where I wouldn't be harassed by scavengers while I tried to figure my next move. A red warning light blazed on the control console, followed by a shrill alarm.

"What is it, computer?"

"An inbound missile rising from the planet's surface," the computer said.

"Launch counter-measures."

"This is a postal carrier ship," the computer said with an element of urgency. "There *aren't* any counter-measures."

"That's disappointing."

"Do something," the computer demanded.

"Bring up the radar display, and give me an ETA for the missile."

The radar image blipped to life on the main monitor. "Inbound missile will impact in forty-five seconds."

I took the stick in two hands and readied myself for evasive action.

"This is your fault, isn't it?" the computer said.

"What? How is it *my* fault that *you* don't have counter-measures?"

"No, I mean you did something to make these people want to kill you, and now *I'm* in danger, too."

"I'm trying to pilot this ship, and you're not helping with my concentration," I said. "Can you scan the missile and tell me what kind it is?"

"The kind that blows up!"

"Computer!"

"I do not possess military software," the computer said. "I have no way to interpret the scanned data. Twenty-five seconds to impact."

I jerked the stick for evasive maneuvers, but the radar blip kept coming for us.

"Ten seconds," the computer said, its volume increasing. "Do something."

"I'm trying!"

"I don't want to die!" the computer screeched. "I still have a year on my factory warranty."

"Shut up!"

"Impact in four, three, two—"

An ear-splitting crack. The ship jerked, threw me hard against my restraining straps. Warning lights of all kinds erupted on the control console. The sky became a blur in the viewports as the ship went into a flat spin.

Circuits overheated. Sparks.

Smoke filled the cockpit.

"Computer, vent the cockpit."

"We're doomed!"

"Vent the fucking cockpit so I can fly this thing."

Fans whirred and the smoke was sucked out.

The ship was heading down fast and spinning out of control. The training kept my mind clear. I refused to vomit, and fought with the stick, trying to stabilize our plummet. My shoulders, neck, and wrists ached. I might as well have been trying to fly a bowling ball through a sky full of mud, for all the control I had.

The computer was… crying.

I broke out in a cold sweat on my neck and under my arms. I gritted my teeth so hard that my jaw ached. Pulling back on the stick with everything I had, I slowly brought us out of the spin, but we were still diving hard, and the ground was coming up fast.

The missile must have been a small one—maybe a shoulder-launched model—but it was enough to fuck the engines. I barely had fifty percent thrust.

"Computer, what's the damage?"

"The ship's fucking broken," it responded. "Are you happy?"

"That's not helpful."

I saw a city, and the ocean beyond. Ditching in the water was probably our best bet, but no way was I making it that far. A second later we were over the city. I spotted a park and a pond and aimed the ship toward it. The angle was too steep.

This was going to hurt.

The ship hit the pond with a smack, water foaming over the windshield, then mud, and then we hit something so hard I was thrown forward, one of my strap buckles snapping. My helmet hit the console, hard, the glass of my faceplate spider-webbing. The impact rang my bell but good, and I blinked, seeing double. Only the helmet kept me from caving in my skull. Warm blood trickled down the side of my nose.

"You... did this," the computer groaned, its power fading. "You... fucking... dick..."

And then I passed out.

NINETEEN

I'd only been out a few minutes. I pried the helmet off and tossed it aside. Dazed. Something warm and wet was on my face. Blood.

A thick layer of gray smoke hung in the cockpit again.

"Computer, vent the cockpit."

Nothing.

Unreliable little prick.

I took off my gloves, wiped the blood out of my eyes.

The front viewport was covered in mud. I wasn't sure where I was. Safely on the ground yes, but what was out there? "Safely" might be a relative thing.

I drew one of the pistols and lurched out of my seat, staggering aft toward the main hatch. Opening it manually, I stepped out and sank waist-deep into pond water. I splashed ashore and saw that the front of the ship had gouged a deep trench into the bank and had slammed to a halt when it hit a huge bronze statue of Heinrich Himmler.

Stumbling out of the water, I went to one knee, panting, head swimming, but I couldn't afford to let my guard down. I took a quick look at my surroundings. A deserted park, empty benches, sidewalks. Litter blew across the landscape, candy wrappers and all the other bright debris of a disposable civilization.

Climbing back into the ship, I took a quick inventory. It told me I had no food, and two pistols with limited ammunition. The wet pressure suit was heavy and cumbersome. I'd need to get back into my regular clothes. My brain shifted into survival mode. I'd become one of the scavengers.

Voices rose in the distance—men shouting back and forth to each other. Searching. The postal ship going down would have been visible for miles, and it had made a pretty good racket when it landed.

I took a deep breath and let the training take over again. I took off in the opposite direction from the voices, moving as fast as I could, and staying quiet.

I skulked along the city's deserted streets, past bodies and burned-out cars, past the remains of a civilization that had collapsed. Then I found a place that might offer something useful.

No such luck.

The police station had been completely looted. There was no clothing or body armor or weapons.

Some of the furniture had been turned over and destroyed, while other offices seemed completely undisturbed. A half-empty cold cup of coffee sat on a desk next to a doughnut with a single bite out of it, as if the owner had only just stepped out to take a leak.

The final room I searched was the radio room. I was surprised to find all of the equipment untouched. The power was out, but I quickly found the backup batteries under the desk, and switched over. I keyed in the Reich frequency for Gestapo headquarters on Mars, and dialed in the identifier codes. I hoped there was a chance that the relay buoys in orbit still might be operational.

I donned the wireless headset, and adjusted the microphone in front of my mouth.

"This is Agent Carter Sloan. If you're getting this, you know who I am and where I am and what my mission is. Except there isn't a mission anymore. Planetary civilization has fallen. I'm stranded and alone. If the Coriandon have overrun the home system, there might not be anyone left to hear this."

I paused to think about that, to wonder why I was even sending the message. Because I was alone. Because maybe the sound of my own voice was the only conversation I was going to get from now on.

"If there's anyone who can hear me, know this. I'm cancelling the mission—or maybe it cancelled itself. Maybe all of humanity is cancelled. Hell, I don't know." I was babbling. "But I'm finished. This is Agent Carter Sloan, signing off."

I took off the headset and tossed it onto the desk next to the radio.

That was as official a resignation as I could manage, under the circumstances. Having done it, I thought I'd feel something—lighter, maybe, or relieved or righteous. I didn't feel a thing. The absolute silence of the abandoned building settled around me like thick wooly fog.

The sudden crack of static almost startled me out of my skin.

"Gestapo coded transmission 66-alpha. Carter Sloan, acknowledge with identification code."

I grabbed the headphones, put them on again.

"I'm here. Hold on. I'm punching in the code now." I typed it into the computer, held my breath.

"Stand by to receive stored message."

"Oh, fuck you." I'd thought I was about to talk to a live person, but I'd tapped into the equivalent of orbiting voicemail. The time stamp said the message was ten days old.

"Carter Sloan, this is Agent Armand," the message began. "The situation has changed dramatically. No matter what happens, the daughter of the Brass Dragon must be kept alive. Repeat: find her and keep her safe at all costs. I will be in contact again, if possible, but the situation back on Mars is dire. We're putting down uprisings all over the place, and the Coriandon are expected to invade any minute. I'll try to arrange some help for you, if I can. Remember the code word SHATTERSTORM. Good luck, Sloan."

The radio coughed static again, and that was all.

I left the police station, heading back out into the lonely rubble of the ruined city.

TWENTY

After the first day, I didn't really notice the bodies. Some had been the victims of violence, stabbed or shot amid the spasms of a dying civilization. Others looked like they'd simply given up, had dropped where they stood in the street or on the sidewalk to lie down and wait to die.

Now they all might as well have been piles of laundry dumped at my feet, shaggy heaps to be stepped over and around. I was too concerned with finding food to care about them. I checked every market and restaurant I passed, but they'd all been thoroughly looted.

Clothing had been hard to find too. I didn't seem to be in a part of the city that had a lot of clothiers. No residences to scavenge either. The neighborhood was lousy with bistros and coffee shops, places that catered to the after-work and weekend crowds.

Finally, in an ice cream parlor, I found something to wear. I'd entered desperate to find food, but my eyes had landed on a pair of mannequins arranged in a quaint tableau. One was a woman in flowing dress, the style centuries old, an open parasol resting on her shoulder. She beamed a coquettish smile at a man, also in period clothing. The male mannequin wore a three-buttoned jacket with wide lapels, wide alternating stripes of red and white. White trousers. Saddle shoes. Red bow tie. The hat was the clincher. An old straw boater with a red band.

I hated myself even as I began to unbutton the jacket, but I didn't have a shirt on under the pressure suit, and it chaffed my nipples something fierce.

The clothes were clean and dry and fit me perfectly. Style be damned. I was garish and bright and clean, relatively speaking.

The ice cream man cometh.

TWENTY-ONE

Next up was some sort of financial district—stocks, bonds, industry. Skyscrapers reaching a hundred stories high. They were a joke now.

I ate a pigeon. Pigeon futures. I'll take a hundred shares. It wasn't really a pigeon. This planet's equivalent. Red feathers. Chewy. Then I found a warm, dry place to sleep, hung up my ice cream suit. The idea that it could get wrinkled or stained was absurdly disturbing to me. I kept the trousers white. I used a rag to shine the shoes each night.

Maybe I should have mentioned the drugs.

Sometimes I heard gunshots in the distance. Always I moved away from the sounds, quietly and quickly. But after two weeks of rat and pigeon and sucking ketchup packets from abandoned fast-food joints, I almost wanted to move *toward* the sounds. Toward people. Toward salvation or damnation. Toward life or death.

My training was the best of its time. Survival wasn't a problem. I could live. Yet there was nothing in my training to make me understand *why* I might want to live.

I spotted the pharmacy on a corner at the edge of the financial district. It wasn't as empty as I thought it would be, and I found what I wanted. Some nights I wanted to sleep, but couldn't. Other nights I needed to stay awake, keep moving, avoid the gunfire. Up. Down. Popping different pills each night. It wasn't unusual for an agent in the field to take drugs and prolong his usefulness. Nevertheless, I was getting frayed, nearing the end.

My body couldn't take much more.

I sat on a bench in what was some kind of theater district. The marquee advertised shows like *Fatherland Follies* and *Nation's Pride*. As the sun went down, I popped a pill to stay awake. I was looking at something specific, and wanted to keep looking.

The gigantic electronic sign down the side of the building was mesmerizing. For starters, it had to have its own power source, because it blazed like nothing I'd seen in days. That's why I wanted to wait for sunset, to see the square lit up. I sat awash in red light, staring at the words DRINK BLITZ COLA three stories high. Then the time. Then the temperature. Then the cola advertisement again. The drugs buzzed through my veins and the sign started to sizzle around the edges.

I grinned.

It was hypnotic.

A public service announcement for a concert in the park. Another for a food drive for the homeless. The cola ad again. The light from the sign bled into the rest of the world, became the world. There was only garish light and meaningless messages screaming out to nobody.

I laughed out loud. The sound was strange in my ears.

Blitz Cola. Time and temperature. A message for Agent Carter Sloan. They may as well have not been words, just blinking designs, hieroglyphics to aliens who might come a thousand years from now, pretty lights to delight a child and—

Wait... what the fuck?

It had to be the drugs.

I sat forward on the bench, rubbed my eyes. I willed the narcotics into the background of my consciousness. I was only partly successful, so my head was swimming, though the delight of the lights and colors completely vanished.

The messages cycled through again, and I'd almost convinced myself I'd been hallucinating when there it was in giant glowing letters.

This is a message for Agent Carter Sloan.
Elimination order reinstated.
Radio ASAP for further details.

I blinked. I sat perfectly still, waiting for the messages to cycle through one more time, and there it was again. *Elimination order reinstated.*

"You motherfuckers."

The walk back to the police station was uneventful. I keyed in my code and received another stored message:

"Agent Sloan, this is Colonel Blake Gideon. Agent Armand is dead. He was killed putting down the rebel uprising here on Mars. First, I wish to assure you that everything is completely in hand here at Gestapo headquarters. Rebel forces have been driven to the outskirts of the city, and order is currently being restored to every zone."

Gideon sounded nervous and was explaining just a little too much. My guess was that things weren't as much "in hand" as he was letting on.

Not that it mattered to me.

"It is more important than ever you eliminate the daughter of the Brass Dragon," Gideon continued. "She abides in the heavily fortified naturalist compound on a remote island. The island is self-sufficient, and we believe it has survived the global collapse of New Elba's society. I've attached a map with coordinates."

The printer next to the radio spat out a color map.

"Proceed immediately to the island and carry out your mission," Gideon said. "The Reich is depending on you. This transmission is concluded."

I keyed in my code and put the headset on, spoke directly and clearly into the microphone.

"Listen, Gideon, it might help to know exactly why this woman is so fucking important. Also, please note I'm not going to be near a radio anymore, so it might be difficult to communicate. Sloan out."

That didn't explicitly say that I was back on the job. Let the bastards think whatever they wanted.

Suddenly I felt an urge to violence, and even though I knew it was the drugs putting me on edge, I couldn't control the outburst. I pulled my pistol and blasted the radio three times. It sparked and smoked, pieces flying all over the room. No more messages from the Reich. Fuck 'em.

I slouched back out to the street, pistol still in hand.

"Where are you?" I shouted. "Come get me! Come get the Nazi, you cowardly shits!"

Not a peep. Not even a hint of breeze.

The planet was as still and as quiet as a tomb.

Or a cryo-stasis chamber.

I turned south and walked toward the ocean.

TWENTY-TWO

I could smell the salt air and the vague odor of rotting fish. I was getting close.

Funny, but I didn't really consider myself to be working for the Reich any longer, and yet there I was heading for the shore, thinking I might need a boat, the map folded neatly in the pocket of my striped jacket. It was the training. There was no turning it off.

But it was more than that. I had to find this woman—not to kill her, maybe not to save her, either. Simply because I had to know. What was it that made her the focus of the Reich's attention? She was just a woman like any other, wasn't she?

I had to know.

Also, I was starving.

I chased a rat down the sidewalk for five minutes

before realizing it was an enormous dust bunny tumbling in the breeze.

I popped another pill. They kept me going, but I could feel my body buzzing with the narcotics, burning itself up. I couldn't keep going this way forever. I needed real food. Real rest, too.

Don't dwell on it, I told myself. *Keep going. Find the sea. Find* her. *Don't ask why. Just do it.*

A dog barked.

I turned, blinked, not sure if I'd heard what I thought I heard. It came around the corner, tongue lolling and tail wagging. It was one of those little, yapping ankle-biters, some kind of terrier maybe. It looked a little thin and scruffy, but not especially malnourished. So far the dog was weathering the fall of civilization better than I was.

It sat in front of me, cocked its head to one side.

"Agent Sloan, I presume," it said. I understood the words, but the voice had a low growling quality.

"Holy shit, a talking dog." I pulled my pistol, pointed at its face. "Explain yourself, mutt."

The drugs. *It has to be the drugs.*

"I'm a Reich A.I. infiltration parasite sent via fast drone from Mars," the dog said.

"No," I replied. "You're a hallucination, and I'm going to shoot you."

"Please refrain," the dog said. "Here, take a look."

The dog spun around, and I saw a little silver disk the size of a coin attached to the base of its skull. A little nub of an antenna.

"You'd indicated you might be out of radio contact," the dog said. "Sending another agent would take too long. A fast drone through the nearest wormhole was the only way to send word in time."

I shook the gun at him. "But why are you attached to a fucking dog?"

"I've been programmed with your smell signature," the dog said. "I am hooked into the dog's spinal column. Powerful microcomputers interpret the scent trail which led me to you. I'm also able to use adjusted voice signals to use the dog's larynx for speech."

"I'll be damned."

"I am not programmed to comment on that eventuality."

"Okay, you found me. What now?"

"The kill order has been rescinded," the dog said. "The daughter of the Brass Dragon must not be harmed."

What the fuck?

"You Gestapo shitheads are driving me insane!" I screamed.

"This is not the intent."

I went to one knee and put the pistol directly against the dog's forehead, right between the eyes. "I think I *will* shoot you." Hate surged in my veins. I felt hot and dizzy. "And then I'll build a fire and cook you. The last thing I want you to know is that you're going to be delicious."

"Please refrain until I transmit our reply to the satellite."

"My reply is *fuck you.*"

"That reply is not relevant to the situation," the dog said. "A Reich battle frigate with a team of shock troops is on its way. Their objective is to extract you and the daughter of the Brass Dragon, once you've secured her. Her safety is top priority."

"Why?" I screamed. "Why why whywhywhy? What is she to the Reich? What is she to *anybody*?"

"Computer models reveal that she is the crux of some sort of societal zeitgeist," the dog said. "A complex analysis of political and social commentary, the flow of online conversation, the underground chatter of the subversive class, pop cultural references—all carry the undercurrent that the daughter of the Brass Dragon is... something."

"*Something*?" I replied. "What's *that* supposed to mean?"

"It's called the Kardashian effect," the dog said. "The term was coined centuries ago to describe a person who is important or popular or interesting, but nobody knows why."

"This is a joke," I said. "It's got to be a joke."

"It is not," the dog insisted. "I am a sophisticated A.I. I understand humor, but am not programmed to use it. All you need to know is that you must secure her safety until the Reich can come pick her up. Everything depends on it."

"*Nothing* depends on it." I spread my hand, indicating the ruined city around me. "There's nothing left to depend on it. Game over, dog."

"This is not within your authority to decide."

I pointed the gun at him. "You're coming with me, and I'm going to cook you and eat you."

"That is not possible," the tiny animal said. "Upon completing my message, I am programmed to self-destruct in three, two—"

"Wait—"

I'd expected an exploding dog to be louder, but it was more of a fuzzy muffled pop. I flinched, bloody chunks and dog fur spattering my shining white pants and striped jacket.

I looked down at the remains of the exploded pooch, tears welling in my eyes. He'd more or less vaporized.

Not a single chunk was big enough to eat.

TWENTY-THREE

I was lost on a boardwalk with carnival games, the booths hollow, tattered banners snapping in the wind. Distorted clown faces on posters, their eyes following me in my drug-induced haze. I wasn't worried about them. I knew I was at the ragged end of my high. I'd crash soon.

No, I wasn't worried about the clowns.

It was the others.

They were coming.

The sound of the exploding dog, muffled as it was, must've drawn them, some lurking band of scavengers. I hadn't seen them yet, but I heard the voice shouting as the mob edged closer, searching for me. I ran, clomping the boards down the midway and turned into a dead end. A huge wooden wall signaled the end of the boardwalk—it was painted with an old-timey mural of some historical scene, tanks with swastikas rolling over fleeing and cowardly men in Russian uniforms.

If I'd been thinking clearly, I might have recalled the battle. Instead, when I looked at the mural from the corner of my eye, the faces of the Russian soldiers all looked like the grinning clowns from the poster. When I looked at the mural dead on, the faces were terrified Russians again. I blinked. Shrugged.

Clowns. Russians. *Fuck 'em.*

I turned to double back and find a way off the boardwalk, but it was too late. They'd arrived, a dozen of them in tattered clothing, rifles slung across their backs. They spread out to keep me from getting past. Their gaunt faces and wild eyes made them look just as hungry as I was.

"What the hell?" one of them grunted, a buck-toothed pilgrim with a wolf-man beard down his throat. "It's the ice cream man."

Even splattered in dog blood, I must have looked like some bright and ridiculous post-apocalyptic harlequin.

"Welcome to the rocky road, you tutti-frutti motherfuckers." It was something I thought the world's toughest ice cream man might say.

There was a prolonged tense pause and then, as if some psychic signal went off, they all charged me at once, screaming and drooling, coming for me with bare hands. From deep within the fog of my narcotic-baked brain, the training emerged. I watched one of my feet spring up and crack the buck-toothed bastard in the face with a rapid kick. One of his buck teeth went spinning away as he spit blood and staggered back.

I used the word *training*, but it was *programming*, every bit as much as the A.I. parasite had been programmed to interpret the dog's sense of smell or use its vocal cords to form speech. I was just a machine that belonged to the Reich, and they were still pressing my buttons back on Gestapo Mars. Instead of circuits and processors, my parts were made of meat and bone.

Oh, sure, I could flip a middle finger to the Reich, say I was my own man, that I'd quit, was out. I could scream it, and yet my feet had turned toward the shore. Find the sea. Find the island.

Find the girl.

As these thoughts rolled around in my head like loose marbles, the programming was still going to town on the scavengers. I spun and shattered a jaw with a backhanded fist. Dropped and swept a leg, upending a man. When I sprang up again, I head-butted another man in the nose, smashing it flat like a rotten tomato, blood and gunk spraying down the front of his camouflage shirt.

"Will somebody fucking grab the guy?" a scavenger yelled.

"We're trying!" another replied.

A wiry guy with greasy dishwater hair and bad skin moved in with a sloppy punch. I caught it, slipped him into a wristlock, and twisted, grinning when I heard the *snap*. He backpedaled fast, screaming and cradling the broken wrist against his chest, eyes wide like he couldn't believe he could get so hurt so quickly.

Then suddenly they all stepped back at once, and I knew that wasn't good. A shadow appeared at my feet. I turned and looked, trying to move aside at the same time, but I was too slow.

A thick cargo net hit me heavy and hard. I stumbled, but the scavengers saw their chance and dog piled me. I looked up through the netting and saw two more of them straddling the top of the wall. They must have circled around and climbed up there while I was pounding on their pals.

At least the pills were working. Fists rained down on me, over and over, and I didn't even feel it.

Okay. Maybe I felt it a little.

Dazed but not out.

I swung in the cargo net like a prize catch, strung between two of the scavengers who carried me as we marched in a line. I drifted in and out, never quite going unconscious.

"Son of a bitch, why didn't we just shoot the fucker?" one of them asked.

"If he bleeds out, he won't be fresh, and we got to wait for the boss and the others," another said. "And anyway, I'm almost out of ammunition."

"I'm out completely." A third voice came from behind us.

They grumbled like that as we marched, the day slipping into evening, and the sound of waves lapping against the shore growing louder. Their gait changed and I twisted my head to glance down through the netting, saw that we were marching across sand now, toward a flickering campfire.

The scavengers carrying me exchanged coarse greetings with those at the camp, and I was dumped into a heap on the sand. I kept still, eyes closed, feigning unconsciousness.

Over the next hour, more of them arrived, and the campfire circle took on something of a party vibe, like some kind of post-apocalyptic beach rave. Going just by sound, I estimated maybe two dozen of them. Then I heard soft footfalls in the sand coming toward me and held my breath.

"Right over here, boss," a familiar voice said. "He's kind of malnourished, but clean. No diseases or parasites, far as I can tell."

I felt someone pulling the net away from me, then a hand on my shoulder turning me over. My eyes popped open and I looked up into the face of a maniac.

Gray hair, shaggy, wild, and blowing in the wind. Eyes bloodshot, fat lips smeared with bright red lipstick, a little golden skull hanging from each ear. A necklace of fingers and ears hung around his neck, his flowered shirt unbuttoned and also flapping in the wind. He looked like a cannibal on a tropical vacation.

He reached down, pinched one of my cheeks.

"Oh, yeah, he'll do," he said, his voice coarse. "You did right to wait for me. You know how I like to hear them scream when they sizzle."

Sizzle?

"Get him up!" the wild man shouted. "I want him stripped and salted and peppered in five minutes."

Then there were many rough hands on my body, jerking me up into a standing position, coat and tie and shirt being ripped away. I got a better look now at the savage faces, hellish in the glow of the campfire. All were snarling and expectant, eager for the carnage to come.

One man stood out among them.

He was huge—tall and fat and nude, and even sitting cross-legged in the sand he was almost as tall as the men standing on either side of him. Skin hairless and rubbery, impossible rolls of flesh in a world without food. At least four hundred pounds. Head like a melon, bald and glistening. His eyes were huge and glassy, firelight reflecting in them. He didn't seem to see anything or even know what was happening. The behemoth sat unmoving, staring straight ahead. He took no part in the revelry and might as well have been some obscene wax statue.

My eyes shifted to the six and a half foot spit they were erecting over the fire. It had a rotisserie handle on one end to turn the meat slowly so it could cook evenly.

The meat.

Me.

It sank in then and I tried to jerk away from the hands holding me. If I could get loose, make a run for it…

"Shatterstorm!" I shouted. "Shatterstorm! *Shatterstorm!*" Maybe there was a pack of Dobermans nearby with A.I. parasites, dogs that could charge to my rescue. Hell, it was worth a shot.

Then there was a movement so slow and subtle, it stood out amid the swarming savagery. The behemoth's gleaming bald head turned slowly toward me, enormous eyes blinking once.

Fists slammed into my body. A shot to the gut doubled me over. Someone grabbed a fistful of my hair and jerked my head up. I was looking into the laughing face of the wild man again.

"Struggle all you want," he said. "It's part of the show. We don't get TV anymore." He turned to one of his minions. "I want a finger and an ear for the necklace, before you put him on the spit. I'm actually getting a pretty good collection and—"

His head exploded.

"Have at the filthy rebels!" someone shouted.

They slammed into the scavengers, a platoon of Reich locals, uniforms frayed but as neatly pressed as possible under the circumstances. Nazis always liked to look their best.

The scavengers returned fire. Bodies on both sides fell. I threw myself to the ground. It would have been ridiculous to get killed by a stray bullet, this close to rescue.

From my position in the sand, I could see both sides merge in hand-to-hand combat. Savages clawed at Reich soldiers. Soldiers stabbed at scavengers with bayonets. Blood and screams.

The behemoth sat there untouched as the battle raged around him, as if he were some inanimate monument. He reached behind his back, stood, and in his hands was a gigantic gun. I say gigantic, but in his fat grip it looked like a child's toy. I knew better. The Mauser-Remington 30mm handheld mini-gun was the perfect weapon for the lone man who needed to kill a lot of foes quickly.

A sweet gun. Seriously.

Shit.

The behemoth thumbed the trigger button, and a storm of lead erupted amid the scream of spinning barrels. Death had arrived, taken a look around and said, *"Let's make a clean sweep of it, shall we?"*

The behemoth wasn't choosy. He swung the gun in a slow arc, slicing through scavenger and Reich soldier alike. Men climbed over one another to get out of the way, battle cries changing to screams of panic and despair. Limbs tumbled through the air, trailing blood. Heads exploded. A Reich soldier standing over me was cut in half at the waist, a chunk of him falling to one side of me, the other chunk to the other side.

A red mist filled the air, and sprayed over everything. My senses were assaulted by the copper smell of blood, cordite, smoke from the campfire. The screams of the slaughtered and the high-pitched whirr of the spinning barrels. The crackling blur of 30mm death filling the air like angry lead wasps.

Then nothing.

It was so quiet so suddenly that it startled me. Waves lapped against the shore. Eventually a few hopeless groans rose from the heaps of the dead and dying.

I staggered to my feet and appraised the carnage. The behemoth stood amid the human debris, face stoic, smoke rising from his weapon. I took a step, my foot squishing ankle deep into the blood-soaked sand. There was nowhere to walk. The beach all around me was saturated with blood and bile and shit from bowels loosened in the final death throes.

So I stopped, stood where I was. The behemoth and I looked at each other, his glassy eyes huge and unblinking.

I cleared my throat.

"That was some fine shooting."

A moment's hesitation.

"Shatterstorm," he said.

Well, fuck...

That had to sink in a moment before I realized the brute was saying the password back to me. I laughed, a giddy relief flooding through me.

"Yeah, Shatterstorm. Why not? Shatter-fucking-storm, baby." I bent over, hands resting on knees, laughing and weak, barely able to stand.

The behemoth dropped the mini-gun and stomped toward me, each step making a sucking sound in the blood-muddied sand.

I stopped laughing.

"Hey there, big fella." I said it the same way you'd talk to a strange dog. A *big* one. "So, what happens next? You call in a Reich ship from orbit, and it evacs us the hell out of here, right?"

He said nothing, didn't even break stride as he scooped me up and threw me over his shoulder. My bare skin against his naked sweaty body was quite possibly the most appalling tactile experience of my life.

"This isn't really necessary," I insisted. "I appreciate the rescue, but I can walk."

He trudged on without a word. Was it was possible he'd forgotten he was carrying me? I might as well have been a rag doll.

"This *is* a rescue, isn't it?"

Nothing.

I thought about struggling out of his grip. He was so greasy and sweaty, I thought it likely I could simply squirt away from him like an errant bar of soap in the shower.

Abruptly, we stopped, and he dropped me in the

sand. I groaned and rolled over. The drugs had been fending off the pain. No longer. All of my bruises were coming home to roost. Ribs, legs, arms, neck, head. Everything hurt. I'd taken a lot of abuse.

The behemoth had carried me further down the beach. Other than that, I had no idea where I was. Maybe this was the rendezvous point for the rescue ship.

I turned my head just a little more and saw the behemoth heading toward a long metal tube. It was maybe twenty-five feet long, about four feet around, half in and half out of the water. At one end was some kind of housing, like for an engine maybe. A propeller. It looked like some kind of torpedo, but seemed too bulky for such a purpose.

The behemoth twisted some kind of lever on the torpedo. There was a *whoosh* of air and a small hatch opened. He turned, waved me to come over to have a look.

Sure. What the hell.

I lurched to my feet, every muscle and joint protesting. I went to the tube, looked inside the open hatch. It was filled with so many good things I wanted to cry. Boxes of fine cigars, bottles of wine and brandy, cans of smoked oysters, jars of olives, cured meats, and the list went on. Some very high-end scavengers had been hard at work. What all this treasure was doing in a big tube I couldn't guess. Maybe this was supposed to be a hiding place.

I turned back to the behemoth, the question plain on my face.

The behemoth gestured to the hatch. "Get in."

His voice rang like something from the depths of a mine shaft.

"Get in?"

He nodded.

"Like hell."

Before I could move he picked me up and began to stuff me though the hatch and into the tube. This time I struggled—to no effect.

There's nothing more discouraging than realizing the man currently trying to manhandle you into a torpedo is actually trying to be gentle. I might as well have been an intemperate kitten he was trying to ease into a pet carrier. He shoved me inside and with one hand held me down between the cigars and a crate of champagne.

With the other hand he put some kind of inoculation gun against my neck and pulled the trigger. Where he'd been keeping it I had no idea. There was a sharp *phump* as something was shot into my bloodstream. Instantly a soothing warmth spread through my entire body, and everything very slowly began to grow dim.

"Oh... yeah."

He leaned in, his face inches from mine, fetid breath like someone had suddenly hit me in the face with a mallet.

"There's been a change," he said.

I wanted to ask what change, but the only sound my mouth could make was "Whaaaa... uhhh..."

"Word came in an hour ago." His voice echoed inside the tube like we were deep inside some ogre's cave. "They don't want to risk it. The girl has to die," the ogre said.

He closed the hatch, and I heard the hiss of air as it sealed shut.

I hate this job.

TWENTY-FOUR

Floating was almost like flying. I glided through a dreamscape of pure darkness, gently turning and bobbing and drifting into a darkness of a deeper kind. Finally there was nothing and nothing and nothing until...

...my eyes...

...popped open.

Everything clean and white. Was this the afterlife?

Would the afterlife smell like antiseptic?

I looked down and saw that I was wearing a white and perfectly starched hospital gown. Lying on clean white sheets. Across the white room was a white door in a white wall. It was like living inside a light bulb.

But I was comfortable and clean and my various aches and pains had faded enough that I could almost ignore them. I took stock. I'd been bathed and shaved, given a neat haircut. There was a tube hooked into one of my arm veins—probably keeping me hydrated. Feeding me nutrients.

The white door opened in the white wall, and a very white woman entered the white room.

She wore a white, form-fitting nurse's uniform, white hose, white shoes. Her skin was so white and clean, it almost glowed. White lipstick and white fingernail polish. She was pretty by default in that her skin was so clear and smooth, there wasn't a single crease or wrinkle or defining feature of any kind. Her hair was a startling contrast to the rest of her. It was a glossy black, slick, and cut short like a boy's. The whole look was so severe it bordered on admirable.

Nazi girl. Should have been on a recruiting poster.

"And how are you feeling, Agent Sloan?" Her voice was crisp and precise. She bit off each syllable like she was trying to punish it for escaping her mouth.

"Better than I deserve," I said. "Last I remember, a naked giant was shoving me into a torpedo."

"That's Rudy," she said. "He procures for us."

"So I discovered," I told her. "I had a first-class ticket between a box of cigars and a crate of champagne."

"Please don't think us spoiled here, Agent Sloan," the nurse said. "He also smuggles in medical supplies and information. This time he smuggled you."

"How long have I been out?"

"Not long," she said. "Not quite twenty-four hours. We've taken good care of you."

"I'm sure."

"Is there anything I can get you?"

"That depends," I said. "Where exactly am I?"

A raised eyebrow. "Probably best if I let Professor Mueller answer your questions." Leaning over, she removed the tube from my arm, then looked me over with an expert eye. "Are you hungry?"

"Starving."

She gestured at another white wall and a panel slid aside revealing a line of men's clothing on hangers. "These are all your size. Please select whatever pleases you. When you're dressed, exit the room and take the hall to the left, through the door at the end. Professor Mueller will meet you there."

She smiled tightly, nodded, turned, and left.

Getting out of bed slowly, I expected weak legs and a light head, but actually felt okay. Rested. They had, in fact, taken good care of me. Whoever the hell *they* were. And they knew my name. I had the annoying feeling I'd ended up exactly where the Reich had intended all along. It was foolish to think anything else could have happened. I was a tool in their hands, to be used as they willed.

I picked a double-breasted gray suit off the rack. It was an old style that had been brought back and recut to look modern. A black silk shirt and a matching black tie. Highly polished black ankle boots that zipped on the side. I felt human again.

Following the nurse's directions, I stepped through the door. The hallway was different from the stark white of the infirmary. Metallic, industrial, like a corridor in the bowels of some space freighter. I walked to the end of the hall and entered through the door there.

This room was different again. Thick exotic rugs.

Wall-to-wall shelves with leather-bound books. An antique desk to one side. A crystal chandelier loomed overhead. The most eye-catching thing in the room was the long red banner hanging down behind the desk. A large swastika was in the middle of the banner, and perched atop the swastika was a fierce dragon, wings spread, scales of polished brass.

The Brass Dragon. A piece of Reich history thought long forgotten.

A small round table waited for me in the center of the room. It was covered with a white tablecloth. White cloth napkin with a gleaming silver spoon on it. A bowl of steaming soup. A single chair.

I sat in the chair, shook out the napkin and draped it across my lap. I assumed the soup was for me. If not, too bad—I was too hungry to resist. I tasted it. Chicken and rice. It was excellent. It would have been easy to slurp down the whole bowl in thirty seconds, but I refused to rush. I felt civilized again and wanted to stay that way.

"We can do better than soup for you later," a new voice said. "The doctor said go easy at first."

I looked up and smiled. "It's delicious. Thank you. Professor Mueller, I presume."

He stood in the opening of one of the bookcases that swung back to reveal a secret passage. He stepped into the room and shut the bookcase behind him.

"A pleasure to meet you, Agent Sloan."

Mueller wore an olive suit with a muted red vest and bow tie—no glitter. Blonde hair shaved close and flat on top. Square jaw and pale blue eyes. Tall but slightly stooped, wide shoulders. Apple cheeks. A wide grin full of long horse teeth.

"Please. Keep eating." He pulled the chair away from the antique desk and sat across the room from me.

I kept eating.

"You have questions?"

I spooned in another mouthful of soup, then shrugged.

"Please. It's okay. You've had a long trip. Through both space and time."

I made a point of not eating the last few spoonfuls of soup. Pushing the dish away, I sat back and wiped my mouth with the napkin.

"Is there something to drink?"

Mueller laughed. "Of course. Sorry for not offering sooner." He stood and gestured at a shelf of books. The book covers were a façade which slid to one side, revealing a small bar. "Gin and tonic? Scotch? Borealan ale? We have a fair selection."

"I could handle a scotch rocks."

Mueller stepped over, clinked ice cubes into a tumbler, then poured scotch over them. He approached me, but stopped short, fully extending his arm to hand me the scotch. I had to stretch my arm to take it. He returned to his seat. It was as if he was trying to stay out of my reach, like maybe he thought I was a coiled serpent that could strike at any time.

He wasn't wrong.

I sipped the scotch. Good stuff. Expensive. I sipped again. What was left of my aches and pains faded a little bit more. I lifted my drink to Mueller, in gratitude.

"Help yourself if you want another."

"Thanks. I will." I sipped again. "I'm curious. Am I a prisoner or a guest?"

Mueller smiled. "That depends on how this goes, I suppose."

I drained the scotch and headed to the bar for more. "Walk me through it."

Mueller *tsked*, leaned back in his chair, and scratched his chin.

"Where to start?"

"I take it this is the island of the naturalist cult," I said.

"That's not what we call it, but yes."

"I was taken out of stasis by the rebels and ordered to infiltrate." If my cover story still held, he might not know the truth. "You must have discovered this, since you know who I am."

If Mueller knew I was really working for Gestapo Mars, then I was likely in real trouble.

"The rebels who broke you out of stasis were operating under a ruse concocted by me and my associates," Mueller said. "You've found your way here by design, because the daughter of the Brass Dragon wishes it."

That was an eye opener, but I didn't show it. At least he didn't seem to know that it was really the Reich holding my leash.

"Sounds like I'd better have another one of these." I splashed fresh scotch over the half-melted ice in my tumbler.

"Yes, perhaps you'd better," Mueller said, "and perhaps I'd better explain."

"Please."

"We knew we needed an agent everyone could trust, and you, sir, are someone the Reich will trust when we send you back on a very special errand," Mueller began. "That's not to say we thought your loyalty was going to be automatic. There were risks of course. But you'd been in stasis for more than two centuries. You were uncorrupted by the status quo."

"I was loyal to the Reich when I went into stasis," I said. "Why would it be any different when I came out?"

"The fact they forgot about you, and left you in stasis for more than two centuries, would seem to me a good reason to question if they deserve your loyalty at all."

He didn't need me to tell him he was right.

"Additionally, the Reich to which you gave your loyalty no longer exists," Mueller continued. "We were once bold leaders and explorers, expanding out into the galaxy. Ever we looked to the horizon, to the next planet, the next star, but now..." He shook his head, frowned. "The once glorious Reich—the explorers, the heroes—have been reduced to a lazy, complacent bureaucracy. It is time for the Reich to be *great* again."

"And you're the man to make that happen." I swirled the scotch and ice in my tumbler, not wanting to drink this one so fast.

"Me, and others of a like mind," Mueller said. "We have labored three generations to bring events to their climax. There are enough of us who believe the Reich can be great again, and now the final, key element has fallen into place."

I tilted the tumbler back and swallowed. The scotch was too good to resist. If I was a prisoner, then this was the best jail ever.

"Key element?" I asked absently.

"The Coriandon, of course."

It was enough to turn my attention from the scotch. "The aliens?"

"Yes."

"I don't see how a hostile alien invasion force is a good thing," I said, watching him closely.

"Do you know how the Reich originally rose to power, so many centuries ago?"

"Every school kid knows that."

"Do you know what was so dangerous about the Jews?" Mueller asked. "Or the gypsies, or the homosexuals?"

I didn't answer. He already knew where he was going. I let him get there.

"Nothing," Mueller said. "Not a damn thing. The notion of *them* is the most unifying concept ever created. In order for the idea of *us* to mean anything, there must be a *them*. The vast majority of people are content to be left alone, and go about their business. But whisper in their ears that somebody else wants them to live their lives differently, and suddenly you've roused a sleeping tiger.

"The people will stand and shout and fight. Why? Because *they* are coming. It doesn't matter who—a different race, sexuality, religion, philosophy. All that matters is that *those people* are coming. And who will protect us now? Who will protect the good people against the bad people? It has been this way for all of history. Vote for us, fight for us, stand with us. Because we are the 'good' people, and they are the 'bad' people—and how can the good tolerate the bad?"

"So what are you saying? That every cause in history was just made up to manipulate the masses?"

"History is the story the old tell the young to explain all the mistakes they made."

"That's jaded."

"That's reality," Mueller said. "I don't want the story of history to be that the Reich faded away like a sigh from a tired old man. I want to make the Reich young again. I want our people to feel they can do anything, go anywhere, that the galaxy is ours for the taking."

"The Coriandon," I reminded him. "Right now they think the galaxy is *theirs* for the taking."

"I'm disappointed, Agent Sloan," Mueller said. "I thought you'd been paying attention."

"I've been paying attention to the scotch." I refilled my glass again.

"We of the Dragon Society arranged a revolution and plunged the Reich into disarray," Mueller explained. "A fat and happy population will always find something to complain about—food prices are too high, the press isn't free enough, too much red tape for abortion vouchers. The slightest inconvenience can be made to seem like the greatest injustice.

"But tell people the problems are the fault of some villain, and you'll win them over every time."

I drained the tumbler, filled it again. It might have been the best scotch I'd ever had. I was vaguely aware that Mueller was still talking.

"These same people will come running for the

government to save them when the chips are down," Mueller continued. "That's where the Coriandon come in. When confronted with godless aliens, the populace will demand protection, and a panicked and ineffectual Reich will have little choice but to accept new leadership. Leadership provided by me, and my compatriots. The failed, gutless, sluggish bureaucrats will make way for a new Reich, reborn in fire and blood. A Reich that will sweep aside the alien scum of the galaxy in favor of human rule."

Scotch. If I kept drinking the scotch, Mueller's voice would fade to smug background noise. The chattering squirrel who meant to take over the galaxy with speeches and propaganda. It was ridiculous.

Then again, maybe it was working. The planet *had* fallen, and I was light years out of the loop. For all I knew, planets were falling the same way all over the Reich. Armand was dead. There was trouble even back on Mars.

I turned back to the scotch for answers. It was worth a try.

Mueller continued as if I were hanging on his every word.

"The people need only one thing more," he said. "A symbol. A focus for their hopes."

"The daughter of the Brass Dragon." I guess I was listening after all.

"Just so," Mueller said. "From the lost line of the original men who tamed Mars. The hardest of them, the most fearsome. A man who spilled oceans of blood to keep the Reich strong and pure. The daughter is a direct descendant."

I gulped scotch, sighed.

"What's all this naturalist stuff anyway?"

"That's what they call us on the mainland." Mueller said *mainland* as if it were a place where the tribal savages lived. "The galaxy is meant for humans. The Reich has let far too many alien species settle within our borders. They bring corrupt ideas."

I had no idea what he was worried about. It wasn't as if we could mate with them and produce bug-eyed half breeds.

"And there's more," Mueller said. "A kind of purity that's far more important. For nearly two centuries, men have been augmenting themselves. Adding metal to their arms and legs to make them stronger and faster. Computers in their heads to make them think better. Humanity is turning itself into one big connected machine, all plugged into the central computer. So what does that mean?

"I'll tell you. It means men and women don't have to try anymore. If they want to be better, they don't have to work for it, don't have to *achieve*. They can just buy a little trinket and plug it in. If a man wants to learn Italian or Chinese or Martian trader dialect, they can just download it right into their brain. Everyone can be equally superior, which means nobody can be anybody, really. Soon there will be no such thing as failure, and that renders success meaningless.

"We're going to give humans back their humanity."

"That's a nice speech and a pretty philosophy." I finished the last of the scotch in my tumbler. It had gone weak with the melted ice. "But you're out of scotch, and now I'm bored."

Mueller chuckled. "So you won't join us?"

"I didn't say that. As you pointed out, the current iteration of the Reich left me to rot in stasis. If you hadn't manipulated the rebels into rousing me, I'd still be there. And I'm flesh and blood, so that should make you happy." Never mind I'd been programmed just as well as any computer. "Let's say I find that my loyalties at the moment are... in flux."

I had to assume the room was equipped with heart scanners and other sensors to monitor blood pressure and pupil dilation, but I was pretty sure I'd had enough scotch to foul the readings. They'd have to do better if they wanted to catch me in a lie. Probably I was just being paranoid, but the scotch really was excellent, so I didn't mind taking the precaution.

"Perhaps we can convince you to remain as our guest," Mueller said. "If you see what we do here, it might nudge you favorably in our direction."

"By all means," I said. "Put me down for the full tour."

TWENTY-FIVE

The central hub of the installation was a great domed crossroad. Two-dozen broad corridors emptied into a central atrium, the glass dome rising multiple stories overhead, blue sky and sunshine pouring in from above. The atrium seemed also to serve as some kind of central meeting place, and men and women hung about in twos and threes, conversing. All wore expensive clothing and eyed us with mild curiosity as we passed.

"Where are we exactly?" I asked Mueller. "I mean, on an island, yes, but what sort of place is this?"

"I'll show you."

He escorted me down a long side hall and we stepped into an elevator. He tapped some kind of code into a keypad and we went up quite a long way, then stepped out onto a long observation platform at the top of a tall tower. The tower was the pinnacle of the main dome, which was surrounded by five smaller domes. It was a big place, bigger still if it extended very far underground.

I looked out past the installation. The island in every direction was made of impassible mangrove swamp, all the way to the sea.

"We like our privacy," Mueller said. "The only way in is through the secret underwater path to the submarine pens. The swamps are far too thick for a landing."

I looked up. "They could come from above."

"And where would they land? Anyway, there's a laser matrix five hundred feet over our heads. Anything that tried to fly in, hoverbots or glider squadrons, they'd be cut to ribbons. And any Reich agent who attempts to infiltrate will be detected because all of the modern agents are corrupted with enhancements." Mueller shook his head. "Not that I'm worried. The rebels are crawling over the remains of the cities, scavenging for food, and the Reich is light years away scrambling to defend itself against the Coriandon."

"Who lives under these domes?"

"The best and the brightest," Mueller said. "Those with resources, and also vision. It's an achievement, this place."

"But it's not enough."

His face very slowly darkened. "No."

"What now?"

"You need to pay a visit to Doctor Turner."

"I thought I'd already been checked, head to foot," I said.

Mueller shook his head. "Not that kind of doctor."

* * *

"I'm Doctor Turner." She stood aside and gestured into her office. "Call me Paige. Please come in."

She wore a gray skirt tight over wide hips. Gray jacket. High-end synthetic cream blouse, clasped at the throat by a mother-of-pearl brooch. Short, only coming up to my chin, wavy auburn hair pulled back into a tight bun. Her eye makeup and lipstick were a matching slate blue, a style I'd seen a few times back in St. Armstrong. She had a sharp angular face which was as severe as it was pretty.

Turner indicated that I should sit on a low, furry couch along the far wall of her office. She sat primly in a swivel chair facing me, ankles crossed, back straight.

"Mr. Mueller told you what I do?" she asked.

"You're a psychiatrist."

"Does that disturb you?"

"No," I said. "Does it disturb you?"

"We're not accusing you of anything," Turner said. "But this is a closed community, living in accordance with certain guidelines. We can't risk a new person introducing a psychosis to the population."

"People here all have their minds right, do they?"

"I'm going to ask you a series of questions," she said. "Just relax and answer naturally."

If you've seen any of the old holovids, you know how this goes. The psychiatrist asks questions—mother, childhood, fears, dreams. Did I hate my father? Did I masturbate? She pecked notes into a compu-tablet until I was beginning to think the real test was to see how much tedium I could tolerate. I answered the questions on autopilot, wondering how long we planned to go on like this.

Dr. Turner set aside her compu-tablet and stood. She pulled a pin from her hair bun and her wavy locks fell down past her shoulder.

"You don't mind some music, do you?"

"I don't mind."

"Computer," Turner said. "Play ambient jazz."

Music seeped from hidden speakers. It had the flow of improvisation jazz, but sounded more like random musicians standing in a loose group each waiting for the other to discover what song they were playing. The volume seemed too high to facilitate meaningful conversation.

Turner sat on the edge of the couch, next to me. "Some of my patients recline. Feel free if it will put you more at ease."

"I'm good," I said. "Not my first time sitting up."

She put a hand on my thigh. "Seriously. I want you to feel as if this is a relaxed environment. A *very* relaxed environment."

I raised an eyebrow.

"As I said before," Turner said, moving her hand farther up my thigh, "we're a closed community here. We see a lot of the same faces, over and over again. It's new and exciting when we have a chance at fresh blood."

Then she removed all possible doubt where her hand was going.

She squeezed.

My pants grew tight.

"Is this some new form of psychiatry?" I asked.

"Let's just say it's therapeutic for both parties." She leaned in and kissed me hard on the lips.

I kissed back. She still had a firm grip on me with one hand, her other one going behind my head to hold me in place, her tongue darting in and out of my mouth. My hands went inside her jacket to cup both breasts through the sheer material. A flimsy, lacy bra underneath. Material too thin to hide her rapidly hardening nipples.

She kissed her way across my face, nibbled my earlobe. I felt her hot breath on my ear as she whispered, "Shatterstorm."

I went stiff when I heard the word.

The other kind of stiff.

Shit.

"I've been waiting and waiting for somebody to come," she whispered. "I think I've removed all of the electronic spy devices, but I can't be sure. I've turned the music up to cover our conversation."

Her hands worked my zipper and pulled me out. She stood, hiked up her skirt and wriggled out of black lace panties, kicked them away. She positioned herself over me, grabbed me again, and put me inside. I bucked my hips and she gasped as I went to the hilt. She quickly found a rhythm, rocking back and forth.

"If there are spying devices," I whispered, "won't this seem suspicious?"

"No." She picked up the pace, her round ass slapping my thighs, a little grunt squeezing out of her on every down thrust. "I'm supposed to examine you, make sure you weren't programmed with subconscious assassination commands, but I'm also supposed to get close to you. Make sure you see things our way, and want to join us.

"I... can be... very... convincing."

She threw her head back and shivered, mouth open, eyes shut tight.

"That's a little one," she said. "I always have one or two little ones before the big one."

I grabbed two big handfuls of her plump ass and thrust as hard as I could. I was heading for the big one myself.

She bent over to whisper in my ear again.

"What are the orders from Mars?"

"Kill her," I whispered back.

"Good," she said. "I've been planning. I've hid away weapons. They have something in mind for you, but I don't know what it is. You need to kill her before they implement whatever that plan is." She increased her speed, humping and humping and humping. "Yes... kill her... yes... kill... kill...

"YES!"

TWENTY-SIX

"Tell me again what all this is about?" I asked.

"A reception. To welcome you," Paige Turner said.

"I like how you're dressed."

She smiled. Her dress was of some fabric that might as well have been mist clinging to her body, red but transparent, her curves plain underneath.

"Typical for this sort of affair," she said. "As is your garb."

I wore loose silk trousers and shirt, a garish pattern of gaudy colors. Pajamas really. Slippers so light I could have been walking on a cloud.

"Come." She took my arm. "Everyone is waiting."

We walked into the reception.

It was a large domed area, not as big as the domed crossroad, and there was no blue sky above, but a slow swirl of festive colored lights. The place had been fashioned to resemble some kind of garden area with grottos and fountains and thick grape vines climbing up trellises. There was something vaguely Roman about the whole setup.

Mueller approached me wearing a similar set of pajamas. He held a silver goblet in one fist and smiled crookedly at me.

"Ah, the guest of honor." He turned to the rest of the throng, lifting his goblet high and gesturing grandly at me with his other hand. "Ladies and gentlemen, may I present the newest addition to our elite community. Carter Sloan."

Polite applause rippled through the throng. Smiles and nods in my direction.

"They all have questions and want to meet you, but don't worry, they won't crowd you all at once," Mueller assured me. "Some of the more important council members might circulate past sooner or later, to welcome you, but there's no pressure. It's a purely social event."

"I'm sure I'll have a good time."

"I guarantee it," Mueller said. "We're a very intimate community, and rather free with each other at parties like this. You should consider it a completely safe environment, and please remember that there's no judgment here. Doctor Turner will be more than happy to show you the ropes, I'm sure." Mueller smiled at us again and drifted back into the depths of the crowd.

Turner took me by the arm and steered me toward a table laden with food and drink. It was strange not to feel hungry, after my time fleeing from the scavengers, but none of the food tempted me. I did happily accept a goblet of wine. A single sip told me it was an excellent vintage. *Score one for the Dragon Nazis*. They knew how to live well.

A servant in a white coat stopped in front of me. He bowed and held a tray toward me. I eyed the unfamiliar offering with skepticism. Neat rows of little pink squares, like samples of bubblegum.

Paige plucked one from the tray and popped it in her mouth, then chewed slowly.

"It's a narcotic produced from natural plant life found on the planet. It retards the areas of the brain that produce anxiety and inhibitions. You'll enjoy the party more if you have one or two. Trust me."

When in Rome.

I popped one into my mouth. It was spongy, but dissolved quickly, making my tongue and gums tingle. At first, nothing happened, so I washed it down with the rest of the wine and filled the goblet again.

A moment later, I looked up.

The swirling lights above me had turned into some sort of bizarre living things, circling the dome like angels of liquid light. A second later I felt myself lift, lighter than cotton candy, and the lights spun around me, caressing my body, and I was light, too, and we all danced together in the sky and—

I blinked.

I was standing on the floor again, the party still unfolding around me. I was a dozen feet from where I'd started, but had no memory of moving. I looked around for Paige.

She stood, eyes wide, head tilted to one side, a

dreamy expression on her face. Transfixed by the color show. A tall man with a neatly trimmed beard stood behind her, one hand up under her dress, snugged casually between her legs. Turner moved her hips in a slow circle in response to the man's attention. Then she reached out to cup the breast of another woman standing close to her.

The nurse who'd tended me earlier.

I looked around. The entire party writhed like a single pulsating sex act, swaying to music, transfixed by the lights, hands and mouths roaming over whomever happened to be handy.

There was a soft pressure on my leg.

It seemed to take an hour to turn my head and look. I was in some sort of sweet foggy paradise. Harsh reality seemed light years away. There was nothing but this place in this moment.

The pressure against my leg was a handsome black woman with impossibly perfect cheekbones. Like all the women at the party she wore a dress of the same ephemeral material. It was golden against her onyx skin. She was tall and athletic and had straddled one of my legs, rubbing up and down like a cat wanting a scratch. As she gyrated, one hand went inside my shirt, long fingers raking through chest hair. She kissed my neck.

The colors overhead flared and billowed and I was lost in a sea of sensation, bliss blurring into bliss, a state of perfect contentment. Sight, sound, taste, smell, touch. All melted down into a new hot glowing element called pleasure.

I think a lot of this happened to sitar music.

* * *

It went on for hours or maybe only minutes. Time became meaningless.

Until suddenly it had meaning again. I blinked, and took stock of my surroundings. I still felt at ease, vaguely euphoric, but I was no longer lost to pure ecstasy.

I looked down to see that I had my pants around my ankles and was taking a short blonde from behind. She was bent over the food and drinks table, eating pudding from a bowl, using only her fingers.

Paige was suddenly at my side. “They pump an oxygen mix into the room to dilute the effects,” she explained. “It means she’s about to arrive.”

“She?”

Turner grabbed my arm to pull me away.

“*Her*.”

Then I realized who she meant. The daughter of the Brass Dragon. At last. I disengaged from the blonde and pulled my pants up.

“Apologies. Duty calls.”

The blonde turned and winked at me. “Next time.” She kissed me softly on the lips.

Butterscotch. The pudding was butterscotch.

Turner dragged me to where the crowd was gathering. I followed their gaze upward, and saw a balcony twenty feet above us. A banner hung from it, the swastika with the dragon perched atop it. I was eager to see her, finally, in the flesh. It was irrational. The woman I was fated to kill—and yet nothing seemed more important than finally glimpsing the mystery which had brought me so far across the galaxy.

Heavy velvet curtains parted and Mueller appeared on the balcony. A murmur fluttered through the crowd and died. Every eye in the place glued itself to him.

He raised both hands theatrically.

"Friends. We've come so far together. Sacrificed much and enjoyed much. We've seen dreams blossom and seen them dashed. We strive on, but now at last, it is our time. We are on the cusp of something incredible. The banners of the galaxy are changing day by day, and we lucky few are the ones to answer the call, the ones to hear the bugle finally sounded. Luck. Fate. Strategy. A combination of so many incalculable things has led us down a path, has set us in motion."

He paused, turning his head slowly, seeming to meet every gaze. "If we don't stand up, if we don't seize this opportunity as it is presented, we are not just cowards. We are traitors." He smiled. "But I know that the heart of every man and woman in this room is true."

Abrupt wild applause.

"I know that we will all rise to the occasion," Mueller continued. "The occasion has arrived. Destiny is upon us. We here are brave enough to admit that terrible things have had to be done. That the obstacle of the old Reich had to be torn down so we could step over the rubble on the path to a new horizon. And so we stand amid the ruin we ourselves orchestrated, among the bodies of strangers. We've ruined worlds. How could we do this? Only one answer suffices. The absolute faith that for centuries to come we will have set the Reich on the right path.

The knowledge that we've taken the long view.

"*You*, my friends, are to be congratulated for this."

More wild applause. After a night of drinking and drugs and uninhibited sex, they liked knowing that their sacrifice hadn't gone unnoticed.

"But you don't want to hear any more from me," Mueller said. "I know who you want to see, and I know why. We live in a time in which blood has almost been forgotten—yet some of us remember, and we are a fortunate people indeed, for our leader can trace her heritage back to the originals. The blood of Gestapo Mars runs pure in her veins. Ladies and gentlemen, I give you the daughter of the Brass Dragon."

The applause this time was thunderous, and shook the dome like an earthquake. Mueller stepped aside, and the velvet curtain parted again.

Then she stepped out onto the balcony.

The applause redoubled.

The daughter of the Brass Dragon was nothing short of a goddess. Her skin was dark and golden. A glossy black braid of hair flowed so long that a tender bot rolled behind her to keep it from dragging on the ground. She wore a glittering silver dress that seemed to reveal everything and nothing at the same time. Her face represented every facet of humanity, almost as if emissaries from every possible gene pool had sent DNA as tribute. She was like no other woman, and yet she was every woman.

She said something, and there was more wild cheering. My mind has been conditioned for retention, to absorb even the tiniest nuance from every situation, but I couldn't tell you what she said. Her words were the music of the cosmos, washing over me, seeping into every bone.

I was in love.

Some of that bubblegum narcotic might still have been in my system.

The festivities started up again, but Paige quickly spirited me away down a darkened side corridor on a sub level of the installation. Her demeanor had changed. She was nervous, constantly looking back as if she feared we'd been followed.

"Where are we going?"

"We're almost there," she said. "I've been preparing for a long time, waiting. You got here just in time. I wasn't sure anyone was coming at all. It's been so long since I've had orders."

"Let's not rush into anything." My head was still spinning from the intoxicating image of the Brass Dragon's daughter. I felt as if I'd witnessed some element of nature, instead of just a woman.

"If we're spotted down here in the maintenance corridors, it will seem suspicious," she said. "So yes, please, I'd like to rush. Here. This door." She twisted a handle and I followed her into a room with some kind of giant pipes crisscrossing in every direction. I felt the hum of machinery through the soles of my feet.

"It's a pumping station," Turner told me. "Everything's automated, so nobody comes in here unless something goes wrong—and nothing ever goes wrong."

She dragged a dusty crate from behind one of the large pipes. It was marked SPARE PARTS and was padlocked. She quickly worked the combination, and the lock popped open. She threw back the lid, revealing a cache of weapons within.

"I didn't know who was coming," she admitted. "If it would be a single agent or a whole team. I wanted to be ready."

I peeked over her shoulder at the contents of the crate. There was quite a selection of rifles and pistols—some military, others civilian. She selected a modest automatic and closed the crate.

She turned back to me, held out the pistol solemnly, like a Pharisee charging an assassin with the demise of a messiah.

I started to reach for the pistol, the training already assessing the pros and cons—12mm, fifteen-capacity clip, a bad bet against power armor, but good stopping power otherwise. A close range pistol best for—

—No.

I pulled my hand back, shook my head.

Turner frowned. "What's the matter?"

"I don't want it."

"Look, I know you're capable," Turner said. "Maybe you plan to do it with your bare hands, like with a Jovian nerve pinch or something, but she'll likely have guards around her. You've been invited to a private audience with her, but I don't know the details."

"That's not what I mean."

"Do you want a bigger gun? Ammunition with exploding tips?"

"That's not what I mean either!"

"I'm trying to help you, Sloan." Irritated now. "Tell me what you need."

"I'm not shooting her."

"I don't care how you do it," Turner said. "Hit her in the head with a fucking hammer for all I care, but now that you're here, things will move fast. The window for completing your mission is rapidly—"

"I mean I'm not killing her at all," I said heatedly.

Turner gasped, took a step back from me.

"What?"

"Look, you haven't been through what I've been through. You don't know."

"You said the order was to kill her. You told me yourself."

"Fuck the damn orders." As soon as I said it I felt the tickle of wrongness at the base of my skull. Every instinct said *obey, soldier on, follow orders*.

No. No.

"No!" I shouted.

Turner flinched, looked at me with fear in her eyes.

I held up my hands. *Easy.*

"Listen to me," I said. "Those orders have been changed so many times they don't mean anything anymore. They were issued by people who are dead, then changed by their replacements, then changed again for God knows what reason, all from a million light years away. It doesn't make any sense. I won't do it."

She stared at me for a long time, eyes wide, mouth hanging open only slightly. I just looked back at her without flinching.

"But... orders," she said finally.

I took her by the shoulders and shook her. "Damn it, we're not machines. We can think. We can feel and reason and resist. *We* are here—not the Gestapo. I'm not murdering another person simply because I have orders. I'm going to meet her. I'm going to try to understand. Then I'll decide what to do. Now are you going to take me to her, or not?"

She trembled slightly, most likely wondering where her world had gone, if she'd ever return to a reality she recognized.

"Yes." It was barely above a whisper. "I'll take you to her."

"Good. Then put that pistol back. I don't want it." She did so, and we left the pumping station.

TWENTY-SEVEN

First we took an elevator up. There was no display to tell us which floor we were on or how far we'd come, but our destination was high above the ground floor. Turner explained that the elevator only went to one place. When the doors opened, we'd be there.

She took my hand. "I'm scared."

"Why?"

"Because I don't know what's going to happen."

"That would seem to be the most common state of the human condition," I said, appalled at how intellectual I sounded. "You're a psychiatrist. You don't know this?"

"You think I'm exempt from normal human fears, simply because I'm an expert?"

"I guess not."

"Knowing what I know makes it worse," she said.

"People come to me for answers. You know what the answer is? The answer is, 'You're fucked and it's all downhill from there.'"

"You should put that in a self-help book."

"This is your fault," she said. "I wanted to obey orders."

"We've been over this."

"The single greatest cause of unhappiness is free will," she told me. "Don't you see how easy and satisfying it would be to give ourselves up to authority? Parents, God, the Reich. The blissful relief from responsibility, knowing that someone else, someone higher up the food chain, is responsible. Knowing that it's all out of your hands, and therefore not your fault."

"You're not a very good therapist, are you?"

She shot me a dirty look.

"So far, you're not much of a spy."

The elevator doors opened. The hall was wide and bright and white—no surprise there. A red light blinked down the center toward the doors at the opposite end, leading us on like we were coming in for a landing. When we reached them a dulcet, androgynous voice seemed to come out of midair.

"Identify please."

"Doctor Paige Turner. I.D. code 32B27G. I have Carter Sloan with me. He should be a recent addition to your databanks."

"Voice pattern recognized. You and your guest are cleared to enter, Doctor Turner."

The doors slid open, and we entered a small anteroom where Mueller waited for us. He'd changed out of his party pajamas and wore a black suit, a patch with the swastika and the dragon over one pocket. He smiled like a politician, and we shook hands.

"Thanks for coming," he said. "We're all excited to move forward." Mueller's eyes shifted to Turner. "Can we have a moment, doctor?"

"Of course." She continued on through the door ahead of us.

Mueller shifted his attention back to me, his demeanor serious. "Please understand that only a very small inner circle of people have access to the daughter. This is a special privilege both for practical matters, since we need you to escort her to Mars, and because she's keen to meet you. You come from an era before the Reich had betrayed its purpose. She wants to get to know you."

"Thanks. I'd like that." As I said it, I realized it was true.

"So you're with us?"

The slightest hesitation, and then I nodded quickly.

"Good. We're glad to have you on board." His voice changed, taking on a conspiratorial tone. "This is big, Sloan. The biggest thing in the history of the Reich. It starts right now."

He ushered me through the next door.

You could only really think of it as a throne room.

It was completely white, but not blinding and harsh like the hallway or the infirmary where I'd woken up. The light was soft and natural, pouring in from the enormous floor-to-ceiling windows that made up the far wall. In the center a throne sat upon a raised dais, and a woman sat upon the throne.

The daughter of the Brass Dragon.

She rose slowly, regally.

On either side of the throne, a man in black power armor stood at attention, each holding a lethal-looking automatic pulse rifle. Their mission was clear. Obliterate anyone who tried to harm a hair on the daughter's head. Relief flooded me that such an eventuality would no longer be an issue.

She glided down the steps toward me, her dress flowing around her more like light than cloth. She was perfect and commanding and her gaze upon me made me feel as if I was the only other being in the universe. She smiled, and I felt light, as if I were made of some cool spring mist. She was anything any person could want—mother, lover, savior, friend. I could get lost in those eyes for the rest of my life.

She lifted a hand as she approached. To shake mine? To embrace me? Some other welcome? Her mouth opened to speak, and I breathlessly awaited the first syllable she would ever say to me.

The room shook with thunder, and blood exploded from her chest. She staggered back, eyes wide with disbelief and betrayal. I didn't even have time to react before another shot took her in the shoulder, spinning her back toward the throne. Blood splattered in every direction.

I looked back to see Paige Turner holding the pistol in a two-handed grip, white-knuckled. Her lips curled back in a feral grimace, teeth white and savage. She fired again and again and again and—

And then suddenly she was dancing, a shaky, jerking jig as fountains of blood erupted all up and down her torso. The rattle of high-powered pulse rifles. The sharp scent of copper and cordite. The armored guards ceased fire, and Turner went down like a marionette with her strings snipped.

I dropped to my knees next to Turner, gathered her in my arms, her blood warm and wet as it soaked into my clothes.

"What did you do?" I demanded. "What did you do?"

She coughed, blood covering her bottom lip. "Or... or... orders."

"You fool. You little stupid fool." My mind scrolled though the first aid techniques that had been programmed into my brain. All useless. Turner's story was coming to an end and nothing in heaven or hell would stop it.

She smiled up at me, white teeth stained with blood.

I wanted to tell her something comforting, something to let her know it hadn't been in vain. That she'd done the right thing—but I didn't want her riding to the afterlife on the wave of a lie. So I returned the smile and brushed her hair back behind her ear.

The light went out of her eyes, and there was only a corpse. I felt my eyes grow hot. They started to ache, and then went moist, and suddenly I had no idea who I was or what I was doing here. Why? The simpler the question, the more impossible the answer.

"Aw shit." The voice came from over my shoulder. I turned my head to see one of the armored guards approaching. He took off his helmet. The guy underneath was remarkable in his pale plainness.

"What the hell? Again? How did she get a pistol in here?"

Mueller spread his hands, and he looked pissed. "You tell me, Jerry. For crying out loud, Turner has been with us since nearly the beginning. How could I know she'd go bananas out of the fucking blue like that?"

"So, you want I should do a cleanup?" the other guard asked.

"No, Duane," Mueller said. "Just leave two dead fucking bodies in the middle of the fucking throne room. Of course fucking initiate a fucking cleanup."

"Okay, okay," Duane said. "Just asking."

Mueller pinched the bridge of his nose and sighed. "Jesus. I mean, come on. How about a break?" He looked up and saw me. "Sorry about that."

I blinked at him, mouth working, trying to say something, but my brain unable to supply the words.

"We haven't had this happen in a while," he said, "so we're caught a tad off guard. We'll get it sorted out."

I let Turner slip from my arms and staggered to my feet.

"Sorted out?" I looked down at the daughter of the Brass Dragon. She'd fallen awkwardly, one arm twisted back beneath her, legs together at the knees then spreading apart. She looked like wax. "Sorted out?"

Mueller gestured vaguely at the men in the power armor. "Duane, take care of this, will you?"

"Right." Duane already seemed bored with it.

Mueller smiled tiredly at me. "You probably have some questions about this?"

"What the *fuck*?" My hands trembled.

"Now that you're in our inner circle, we were

going to reveal our secrets... but gradually," Mueller said, and he looked around. "I think we'll need to accelerate the timetable a bit under the circumstances."

Behind him a hatch opened in the wall. Two robots emerged like little bulldozers. They rolled across the floor, scoops lowering, and pushed the two corpses across the floor. Thick red streaks trailed behind them.

"The daughter of the Brass Dragon is too valuable to our plans," Mueller continued.

Another hatch opened on the far wall and the robots pushed the bodies into it, the hatch immediately slapping shut again. Other robots had already moved in to scrub the blood from the floor.

"So naturally, we've taken the appropriate precautions." He gestured at another large section of wall that was sliding back to reveal a hidden room. A line of six-foot glass tubes could be seen within, each vertical container hooked to cables and machinery. The thrum of an electronic heartbeat pumped through all of them. A nude woman floated in each tube, eyes closed, sleeping peacefully. Exact replicas of the daughter of the Brass Dragon.

"Clones," Mueller said.

I blinked at the glass coffins, the women inside waiting for the breath of life if they were needed, like Christmas wrapped dolls waiting to be played with. Duane moved to one of the consoles, tapping instructions for the computer to bring one of the daughters online.

"We wanted to work with authentic DNA," Mueller said. "We tracked down a direct descendant, and keep her in the detention area on one of the sub levels. Clones are easier to control obviously. Too dangerous to use the real girl. It will take a few minutes to download the memories into a new clone and charge the hypno-emitter, and then we'll be up and running again."

My mouth felt dry, and my head was spinning. I gathered myself enough to speak.

"Hypno-emitter?"

"A little gadget we put into each of the clones," Mueller said. "It emits a subliminal wave that causes people within the clone's radius to see her as godlike. It's the real reason we don't allow brain implants, since they could easily filter out the wave. We've spent a long time turning her into a powerful symbol. Those close to her need to *feel* she's special, on a visceral level."

"Fake," I said. "It's all fake."

"Of course it isn't," Mueller said irritably. "It's real because we *say* it's real. We've made it that way. It's the reality we've created. The one we'll enforce."

I was rapidly recovering, my mind clearing. The training was good for something. I measured risk, considered alternatives as I absorbed all of this new information. My mind was a sharp and agile instrument which came up with a plan.

I needed to get the fuck out of here.

TWENTY-EIGHT

They let me go back to the modest quarters I'd been assigned, to make ready to implement their plan. Using my contacts and authority, I was to help one of the clones infiltrate the most secure levels of Gestapo headquarters back on Mars, positioning her for the coup, while armed men and women waited for the signal. It would all happen quickly.

Blitzkrieg.

I had other ideas.

Arriving in my quarters, I changed back into the suit I'd picked out in the infirmary. I would have preferred a survival suit, but anything was better than the pajamas. Then I took the elevator to the same sublevel I'd gone to before with Paige. I paused at a safety station where a fireman's axe hung next to an extinguisher and a first aid kit.

I took the axe.

The corridor was deserted, and nobody saw me enter the pumping station with the axe resting casually on my shoulder. I knocked the padlock off the weapons crate and tossed the axe aside.

Opening the crate, I examined my options. There was a variety of pistols, but I chose a pair of giant 12mm automatics for the simple reason that they came with dual shoulder holsters and plenty of extra magazines. I took off my jacket and strapped them on. There was a little beamer with a thumb trigger, too. I strapped that to my belt. There were a few long-range rifles and street sweepers, but they'd only draw attention as I tried to make my way out of the complex.

Which presented another problem. I'd need some kind of boat or submersible. I hadn't been conscious when they'd brought me in, so getting off the island wouldn't be easy.

Back out in the corridor, I caught an elevator and went down another level. The corridors were lined with exposed pipes and wiring, and there was a constant hum of machinery. There was a framed map on the wall, on it a red star with the words YOU ARE HERE.

If I turned right, the corridor would take me to the submarine pens. I had no idea what sort of security to expect, but I was going to need some sort of transportation. A left down the other way would take me to the detention center.

I mentally scrolled back through my conversation with Mueller.

"*We wanted to work with authentic DNA,*" he'd said. "*We tracked down a direct descendant, and keep her in the detention area on one of the sub levels."*

Somewhere in a cell, a woman was being kept prisoner for no other reason than the accident of her birth. I moved toward the submarine pens, then stopped. My conscience kept tugging me in the other direction. I remembered the clean, simple sense of satisfaction knowing I'd helped Max and his family escape. It was something I'd done, not because of orders or because I was compelled by programming, but simply because I'd understood in some basic way that it was the right thing to do.

I also had the gut feeling that every second was precious. Detouring to find a woman I'd never met, who might not even *be* there, was a bad bet. I couldn't waste a minute if I wanted to save my own hide. The only smart thing to do was head for the submarines as quickly as possible.

I turned back toward the detention center.

Fast-walking, I passed a number of doors on the way. I remembered Turner telling me the whole place was basically automated, so with luck I wouldn't run into anyone at all. Then I rounded the corner and saw a man sitting behind a counter. Behind him stood a doorway with the words DETENTION CENTER on a sign. I approached slowly.

Smiling.

Everything normal.

He stood slowly, eyeing me suspiciously.

"Sir? I'm not sure you're supposed to be down here."

"I'm the new guy Mueller brought in," I said. "He told me I could get a look at the prisoner."

The guard frowned. "Nobody told me. I'll need to check. Do you have identification?"

"Of course." I reached back like I was going for my wallet. Instead, I unclipped the beamer from my belt and brought it around, thumb hovering over the trigger.

He must have recognized it, because his eyes went big.

"Take me back there," I said. "To the girl. No alarms. No heroics. Right?"

He nodded. "Right."

He led me down the main hallway, lined by white doors with little windows and a keypad on the wall next to each one. He took me all the way to the door at the end.

I pointed the beamer at him. "Step back."

He stepped back.

I sidled up to the window and looked into the cell.

Antiseptic white, harsh fluorescent lighting. A small figure lay curled on a cot against the far wall, her back to us. White shorts, T-shirt, and deck shoes. A black braid hung down over the side of the cot. It was nowhere near as long as the clone's exaggerated hair.

I looked back at the guard. "Open it."

"I can't," he said. "It takes an override from Mueller."

"Okay. Put yourself in that other cell over there."

He did, and closed the door behind him. I pressed LOCK on the keypad and the indicator light blinked from green to red. Then I went to the girl's cell and aimed the beamer at the lock. I thumbed the trigger and the red beam began cutting. Where it hit, it sparked, smoked, and popped.

I drained nearly half the charge, but the door finally popped open.

An alarm sounded. Red lights blinked.

If I was in a hurry before, I was twice in a hurry now.

I pulled the door open.

She'd backed herself into a corner, eyes big and afraid, one arm up out of reflex to fend off whatever was coming. She had the same olive skin and Eurasian features as the clones, her long hair braided tightly in the back, but these attributes were no longer mesmerizing. She wasn't putting out the vibe of a goddess. She was just a simple pretty girl, and very afraid.

I clipped the beamer back on my belt, held up my hands, palms out.

"Easy."

"Who are you?"

"I'm Carter Sloan. You don't know me, but I can take you away from this place."

Distrust flashed in her eyes, and I wondered how long she'd been here, what they'd done to her.

"The alarm is sounding, and I don't have time to force the issue," I told her. "I'm not going to drag you kicking and screaming—we'd never make it. We might not anyway. Your choices are to come with me or stay here, but I've got to know right now."

A second of thought, then she nodded quickly.

"Great. Follow me."

We raced from the detention center. I glanced back only once to make sure she was still there. She stayed on my heels, some of the fear on her face replaced by determination.

"What's your name," I shouted back.

"Cindy," she responded. "Where are we going?"

"The submarine pen."

"Where's that?"

"I don't know," I said. "I'm following the signs."

"This rescue seems a little... improvised," she said.

"It was a late addition to my itinerary," I admitted. We came to a metal hatch with an iron wheel in the middle. There was a sign next to the hatch.

SEA LEVEL MONITORED WITHIN.
DO NOT OPEN HATCH IF LIGHT IS RED.

The light was green.

I twisted the wheel and swung the hatch open. We rushed inside. I swung the pistol around, looking for somebody to shoot.

The walkways were barely six inches above the water. My guess was that tides played hell with the water level. The place smelled like sea salt. There were four lanes, three with sizable submarines in them and the last with a much smaller submersible. A gigantic steel door—which I presumed led to the sea—was closed.

A man in a Dragon Nazi uniform appeared atop one of the submarine conning towers. He looked down at me and frowned.

"Sir, are you supposed to be here?"

I shot him through the left cheek. He screamed and tumbled off the conning tower into the water.

The pistol's thunder made Cindy scream, too. "What are you doing?"

"Shooting Dragon Nazi motherfuckers," I said, "and stealing a submarine."

Another guard appeared, looking aghast.

"Oh, my God! What did you do that for?"

"Burn in hell." I squeezed the trigger three times, and he went down in a shower of blood.

"Stop that!" Cindy shouted.

"Just shut up and be rescued."

I ran toward the smaller submersible, assuming she would follow. Another uniformed Dragon Nazi leapt in front of me to bar my way.

"Sir, calm down, I don't think—"

"Eat lead, fascist!" I gunned him down where he stood.

Another opponent rose to take his place.

"Sir, this is a restricted area. Please stop—"

I gunned him in the belly. He curled into a ball as he fell, mewling for mommy.

Cindy screamed again.

"Oh, my God, Arnold!" Another Dragon Nazi ran toward his fallen comrade. "Somebody get the first aid—"

The pistol bucked in my hand. Bullets flew. Flesh shredded. He died down in the everbearing roses.

I felt Cindy's hand on my arm, tugging urgently.

"Stop it," she pleaded. "What are you doing? Stop it!"

I spun, fixed her with a hard look. "What do you think this is? Do you think this happens clean? That we sneak out of here and laugh about it over champagne? These people killed the entire planet." I grabbed her by the hand, held on tight. "Hang on or by God, I'll drag you out of here."

We ran together, leaping over the corpses of the Dragon Nazis. She almost stumbled, then regained her balance. The alarm blared and the red light blinked and reflected off of the water. We passed the big submarines and kept going. I pulled her along frantically, sure that armed men would arrive to bar our escape. I expected a bullet in my back any second.

We sped across the gangplank to the small submersible and climbed through the hatch. I slammed it shut behind us. We scurried forward and took the two seats in front of the big bubble window. I scanned the submersible's controls, began to flip the switches for the startup routine. Another switch, and the big doors to the pen began to slide open ahead of us.

"What are you doing?" Cindy asked breathlessly. "Can you pilot one of these things?"

I chuckled. "Madam, I am a Reich spy of the highest caliber, trained to operate anything that flies, rolls, or floats. My observational and intuitive skills allow me to deduce the operation of this submersible in a matter of minutes. We'll be underway in no time. No problem."

Approximately ninety seconds after that, I wrecked the submarine.

TWENTY-NINE

Wrecking the submarine wasn't entirely my fault. We'd just cleared the submarine pen when they launched the depth charges. Instantly leaks began spraying everywhere.

We surfaced about forty yards offshore, threw open the top hatch and left the submersible behind. It was still taking on water as we waded ashore, the surf crashing on our backs.

"We've got to head inland and hide," I said. "They'll be on us any minute."

Cindy threw herself down on the sand, coughing up seawater. "Just… I need a minute."

"We don't have a minute. Come on!" I grabbed her under one arm and dragged her to her feet, then dove into the tree line, pulling her after me. Thirty yards in and we hit the swamp, sinking knee deep into brackish water, the mud below sucking at our feet. It was slow going, but I kept urging her to keep up.

"Where are we going?" she asked.

"No idea," I said. "We're just trying to put some distance between us and them."

"Are there things in this swamp?" she asked. "I mean... like animals? Like snakes?"

"Lady, I know jack shit about this planet and its local plant and animal life, but I know what a 12mm round with an exploding tip can do to human flesh, so keep running."

We forced our way through a line of shrubs with long, razor-edged leaves. When we came out on the other side, Cindy had a dozen shallow red streaks across her bare legs and arms. A cloud of biting flies attacked us a little while after that, and before long we found ourselves chest deep in dirty water.

"This is impossible." She sounded wiped out, like she wanted to give up. "We'll never make it."

I turned, took her by the shoulders, looked straight into her eyes, so wide and vulnerable.

"We don't know anything about this swamp except that it's big, and I'm not exactly sure where we are. We might be hopelessly lost, or we could come out on the other side any minute. If we can find the beach on the other side there might be a boat. We don't know, but we'll *never* know if we just quit. If you fall over dead, then you'll have my permission to quit, but while you've got breath in your body then you'll keep moving. You hear me?"

Something rallied, her expression hardening. Maybe it was because she'd been a prisoner before, and now she saw her chance to be free. Whatever the reason, she was ready.

"Okay."

We slogged through until the swamp sludge was only over our ankles and we could move faster. Then I stopped abruptly, held up a hand for silence. An electronic whine came to us through the swamp, getting closer. I drew one of the pistols and thumbed off the safety. Cindy looked at me, brow furrowed.

I put a finger to my lips.

A second later, the sniffer emerged from beneath the low hanging branches of a mossy tree. It floated in the air, a shiny metallic sphere the size of a volleyball. It rotated toward us, its single cycloptic camera lens focusing on us.

I lifted the pistol and fired, the racket sending a flock of swamp birds into the air. The sniffer sparked and smoked where I'd hit it, sputtered, and dropped with a plop into the swamp water.

Cindy had latched onto my arm.

"What the hell was that?"

"Sniffer. Tracking us from our DNA trace."

"Did it see us?"

"Without a doubt," I said. "They'll know exactly where we are. We've got to move. Fast."

We tripped and stumbled on through the swamp, filthy and wet. It seemed to go on forever. Cindy would have dropped in her tracks if I wasn't pulling her along.

Then I heard them. I looked back and saw the uniforms through the foliage. They were gaining. I fired at them until the magazine was empty. A body fell, but another half dozen came into view.

I reloaded. Fired again.

A smattering of return fire. Nothing earnest. Another squad of them were coming up on our left flank, and we altered course away from them. I realized too late what was happening.

They were herding us. I couldn't guess what might be ahead, but wanted no part of it and began calculating a new course that would take us out of the swamp, but away from whatever trap they were setting.

Except I was too late.

We burst into a small clearing, and they were waiting. Three of them in bulky power armor. Whoever had modified the armor for the swamp had done a good job. There was a layer of rubber over everything to ward off the moisture. Even more impressive was the stilt modification to facilitate maneuvering through deep water. The men in the armor took long, loping steps and towered ten feet over us.

I pulled both 12mm automatics and blasted away, but the shots sparked and ricocheted off the armor. Hands shot out, the arms extending their reach to grab us. Metal tentacles wrapped around Cindy and she screamed. I fired until I'd emptied both pistols. No effect. The other two armored stilt men grabbed for me. I ducked and rolled through the mud, came up with the beamer, looking for a weak spot. I would have paid top dollar for a shoulder missile.

I fired the beamer at a seam between the shoulder and arm. It flared bright as the metal heated, but otherwise had no effect.

The metallic arms extended, coming right for me.

More Dragon Nazi troops entered the clearing from all sides.

Nowhere to run.

An enormous scaled head dipped down into the clearing, jaws wide, gigantic fangs gleaming with saliva. It clamped tight onto the torso of an armored man, sparks flying as the monster's teeth penetrated armor. There were screams and static as the giant reptile shook the man and then finally flung him dying into the muck.

Two more reptiles rumbled into the clearing, each step shaking the ground. Three of them. A dozen feet high at the hip, looking like tyrannosaurs. A black-clad man with a swastika on his back clung to a saddle on the back of each lizard, reins clutched in one fist, the other hand holding a ten-foot shock lance.

The remaining two men in stilt armor turned away from Cindy to face the newcomers. Shoulder-mounted mini-guns spun into action, spitting fire and peppering the monsters. They roared fury, jaws clamping and sinking into the armor as if it were aluminum foil. They tore the stilt men apart, pieces of them splashing into the swamp.

The other Dragon Nazi soldiers opened fire. One of the huge lizards swung a tail. It slammed into a half dozen soldiers, knocking them back twenty feet, the sounds of screams and snapping bones filling the clearing.

I grabbed Cindy, pulled her out of the way as another lizard chased the remaining soldiers back into the swamp, the creature's roar drowning out every other sound. One of the riders reined in his ride next to us. He removed his helmet and looked down at me and Cindy from his perch.

"Captain Harold Prince of the Eight-Oh-First Mobile T-Rex Troopers, sir. Are you Carter Sloan?"

In my peripheral vision, I saw more of the huge beasts moving into the swamp, mopping up what was left of the Dragon Nazis.

I looked at Captain Prince, eyebrow raised.

"T-Rex troopers?"

"Yes, sir," Prince said. "Bio-engineered from authentic DNA and bred to be domesticated. Much better for terrain like this than mechanized vehicles." He twisted in the saddle and pointed behind him. "Sir, if you go two minutes in that direction, you'll hit the beach. We have a landing platform a thousand yards offshore. It was the only way we could get in under the laser matrix. A boat will take you out to the platform and a shuttle up to the *Pride of Nuremberg* which is waiting in orbit."

I pulled Cindy close to me. "Captain, this woman is important. She has to come with me."

"Understood, sir. Please proceed to the beach."

The roar of the T-Rexes mixed with the screams of the dying Dragon Nazis. We turned and ran, hope and relief giving new energy to our tired legs.

The swamp opened into a wide beach, and two men in Reich uniforms waved us toward a small hovercraft. I glanced down the beach and saw another squad of T-Rexes wading ashore. My guess was that they intended to make short work of the Dragon Nazi installation. Whatever defenses Mueller and his pals might be able to mount, I doubted they'd stand up long to enraged dinosaurs. No more clones, or sex parties, or hallucinogenic bubblegum.

A part of me will miss that, I thought wistfully.

The hovercraft carried us across to the gigantic landing platform. It bobbed gently on the calm sea. The platform rested on several dozen rows of inflatable durafiber tubes, each three stories high. The hovercraft took us around to where an elevator took us topside.

A shuttle was just lifting off as another approached to land. A man with sergeant stripes on his uniform had to shout over the engine noise.

"This is your transport, sir. It'll take you to orbit."

"Thanks," I shouted back.

Cindy and I boarded and strapped ourselves into adjacent acceleration couches. Ten seconds later, we launched, the thrust pushing us back into our seats. We reached orbit, and there was an odd moment of weightlessness until the artificial gravity kicked in.

A woman in an officer's uniform came back from the cockpit to check on us.

"The planetary assault frigate *Pride of Nuremberg* has orders to take you to rendezvous with the rest of the fleet, Agent Sloan." She handed us two plastic bottles. "In the meantime, you might need to rehydrate."

"Fleet?"

"What the admiral could gather from the outer planets," she said. "The rebellion is over. Now we're putting everything we have into a counteroffensive. One final battle."

"Where's the fight?" I asked.

"Mars," she said. "I've got to get back up front and fly this crate. You guys just sit tight and relax."

We were both filthy and exhausted. We cracked open the plastic bottles and drank greedily. Some sort of electrolyte-enhanced mix with a slight lemon flavor. Cindy finished her drink and smacked her lips, then leaned her head on my shoulder, unable to keep her eyes open.

"I never thought we'd get out of that swamp," she murmured. "Thank God it's all over."

Over? I took one of her hands in mine, squeezed it comfortingly. No, nothing was over. Not yet. But I didn't tell her that.

No point ruining it just yet.

THIRTY

They welcomed us aboard the *Pride of Nuremberg* with all courtesy. Nobody asked about Cindy. It seemed enough that she was with me. They gave us each a small stateroom and a change of clothes. We'd have time to rest in the few hours it would take us to reach the fleet rendezvous point.

Again I was reminded of the restorative powers of a hot shower, aches in my neck and shoulders and legs fading as I stood under the hot spray. I was given a jumpsuit similar to the one I'd worn last time I'd been a guest of the Reich navy—black, swastika over one pocket, the words *Pride of Nuremberg* stitched onto one shoulder. I'd just zipped it up and was combing my hair when the door chimed.

"Come in."

The door slid aside and Cindy entered. She wore

one of the ship's jumpsuits, too, sleeves rolled up. It was slightly baggy on her. Her hands were deep in her pockets, shoulders slightly slumped, her body language screaming *awkward*.

Nothing like the clone and its regal fakery. She was real and shy and had no idea what to do now that we weren't running for our lives. She'd also taken her hair out of the long braid down her back and had fastened it into twin pigtails. They made her seem girlish and innocent, and I really didn't know a thing about her, but was glad anyway.

She smelled like soap.

"How are your quarters?" I asked. "Comfortable?"

She shrugged. "I guess. But small—reminds me too much of my cell. And I don't really know anyone on this ship."

"You don't really know me either."

She laughed. "I'm hungry. What about that?"

"Follow me."

The ship's galley was between shifts and nearly deserted. We sat by ourselves at the end of a long table.

Cindy hunched over a bowl of chili, spooning it into her mouth like she hadn't eaten in years. She kept glancing up at me, slightly embarrassed that she was eating like an animal but not quite able to stop herself.

I ate a salad and a piece of lean chicken breast. What I really wanted was three slices of deep-dish pizza, but my training insisted that my body stay fit. I wasn't on vacation. Without a doubt there were more hardships ahead. I would probably have to belt somebody in the face sooner or later. Best to be light on my feet.

Cindy crumbled crackers into her chili, then stirred.

"Where do you think they keep the dinosaurs?"

I blinked at her. "What?"

"Do you think there are holding pens on the lower decks?" she asked. "Something like that?"

"I don't know anything about it," I said truthfully. "They probably keep them in stasis until they're needed. Easier than shoveling a ton of dinosaur crap every day."

"Oh." She looked crestfallen. "I hadn't thought of that!"

"Is something wrong?"

"I was a veterinarian's assistant back home," she said. "I was attending the university, hoping to get my grades good enough for vet school."

A job? Did she think she could get work tending the T-Rexes? But it made me think. With an entire galaxy in upheaval, what did a young veterinarian's assistant do? What was her place? Multiply this dilemma by billions of displaced people on worlds scattered across the Empire. This was the result of the Dragon Nazi's revolution.

"God, I must sound so stupid." She hunched over her chili again, eyes down, shaking her head. "As if taking care of a cat or a parrot is the same as working with dinosaurs."

Every word she uttered broke my heart just a bit more.

I stood, picked up my plate.

Her head came up quickly. "Where are you going?"

"To get some pizza."

The *Pride of Nuremberg* dropped out of translight in the middle of a ragtag fleet. The captain of the frigate allowed Cindy and me to observe from the bridge. Everyone seemed nervous, as if there was some doubt the fleet would actually be there.

A flurry of communications went back and forth between the frigate and the other ships. I ignored the confusion and instead rallied all my powers of observation, studying the fleet through the forward viewport as well as absorbing information from the various computer monitors around me.

The fleet was eighty-seven ships strong. Not bad at first blush, but the reports that flooded in told the whole story. Twenty-two of the ships were legitimate fighting vessels—frigates and destroyers and one light cruiser. They'd been on deep patrol and had remained unscathed by the Coriandon encroachment. The rest of the spacecraft were a mishmash. Police ships from local systems, home and reserve vessels. Ancient freighters retrofitted with translight drives and missile batteries. These accounted for at least a dozen of the vessels. Anything that could fly and shoot had been commandeered to the cause.

One spacecraft above all was simultaneously most surprising and most inspiring. The battle hulk looked like it had been through hell, and I should know. I'd been there when most of it had happened. It looked patched and mended using mismatched metal from a dozen different ships. A tremendous stretch of hull from some other ship—a large troop transport, by the look of it—had literally been welded along the starboard side to cover some massive damage.

Against all odds, Admiral Ashcroft had saved his ship to fight another day. As if summoned, his face appeared on the big forward monitor. Somebody had done a quick cyborg job on the left side of his face, left eye a glowing red light, cheek and ear replaced by gleaming metal. If we lived through this, doctors could supervise a flesh replacement.

"Captain, I understand you have Carter Sloan with you," Ashcroft said.

I stepped up and offered the admiral a two-finger salute. "Right here, Admiral. If you don't mind my saying it, you're a sight for sore eyes."

Ashcroft's grin was lopsided because half his face was metal. "Never expected to see you again either, Sloan. I guess we're both harder to kill than the fates expected. I've arranged to have you transferred to my ship, if that's okay with you."

"I'm traveling with someone," I said. "Okay to bring her?"

"We can accommodate anyone you bring. Sadly, we've lost a lot of crew," the admiral told me. "So space isn't a problem. I'm sending a shuttle now."

The landing bay of the battle hulk still looked like hell, thanks to my hot start in Meredith Capulet's luxury yacht—scorch marks on the deck and bulkheads—but repair crews had made it functional again.

They'd taken on a lot of refugees. A rummage sale variety of smaller ships littered the bay, and there was barely enough room for our small shuttle to park. The doors sealed, oxygen pumps filling the hangar with atmosphere, and Cindy and I were down the gangplank ten seconds later.

Ashcroft was there to meet us. In person, I saw that the cyborg job wasn't limited to his face. His left arm was made from the same shiny metal that was on his face.

"I was lending a hand down a maintenance conduit when a missile slammed right into us," Ashcroft explained. "They pulled me out and patched me up. I told the doc to slap on whatever spare parts were handy, so I could get back to work."

"Hats off to your doctor *and* to your repair crews," I said. "I felt sure I'd seen the last of this ship."

"Repairs have been constant," Ashcroft said. "Lucky for us we managed to get some extra help. I believe you know this gentleman." The admiral gestured, and I looked behind me.

"Max!"

He wore the same black jumpsuit as the rest of us, a toolbox in one hand. We shook hands, slapped each other on the back.

"This is amazing. How did you end up here?"

"The fleet picked us up just outside the system," Max said. "I've been lending a hand." He turned to Ashcroft. "Admiral, last time I saw this man he was taking on an entire mob of scavengers to cover our escape. The fact he's here is nothing short of a miracle."

"I think Mr. Sloan must be in the miracle business," Ashcroft said.

"And the family?" I asked. "Everyone's safe?"

"We all made it," Max said. "Thanks to you."

"That's fantastic," I said. "And what about… I mean did *everyone* make it? Did—"

"I'm right here, you sonuvabitch."

I turned when I heard her voice, and smiled.

Meredith threw herself into my arms and we both hugged so tightly that it seemed impossible we'd ever let go. She turned her thigh to rub against the bulge in my pants. After a long time, I felt everyone else's eyes on us and disentangled myself. I noticed that one side of her head had been shaved, a metal disc the size of a small coin above her ear.

I frowned at it. "What's that?"

"Long story," she said. "I'll tell you later."

Cindy hung at the edge of the conversation, hands clasped shyly behind her back.

"Everyone, this is Cindy," I said. "She's been to hell and back like the rest of us. I guess we're all survivors." Never mind who she was. That wasn't something I planned to mention until I figured out if I wanted to mention it at all.

Cindy and Meredith exchanged appraising looks, Cindy timidly from the corners of her eyes, Meredith like she was picking out something to cook and eat.

"I hate to break up this happy reunion," Ashcroft said, "but I'm hoping you can help me, Sloan. Can I get some of your time?"

"Of course."

"I'd better get back to work, too," Max said.

"Catch up with you later."

Meredith put a hand on my arm, and made sure Cindy saw her doing it.

"I'll come to your quarters later and... catch you up on current events."

"Good. See you soon."

"Follow me, Sloan, and I'll put you in the picture." Ashcroft headed for the elevator across the hangar bay. Cindy stuck close to me, a thin nervous shadow.

We followed the admiral to the briefing room just off the bridge and stood around a circular holo-table. He punched up the display he wanted and a color 3-D image of our sector of the galaxy blipped to life in front of us.

"Obviously this is Mars." Ashcroft indicated the red planet on the display. "Reports indicate that the Coriandon are moving slowly and methodically through the system, taking out Reich outposts. They don't want anyone behind them when they make their assault, and the Reich doesn't have enough ships in the system to stop them. All they can do is pull back, wait for the attack, and defend the home world the best they can."

I scanned the readout display, which conveyed the particulars of the invading fleet. "That's not necessarily an overwhelming number of enemy ships," I said. "There's a good chance Mars can hold out."

"Normally I'd agree," Ashcroft said, "but intelligence reports two more Coriandon fleets massing at wormholes here... and here." He indicated the points on the display. "Mars can't withstand that kind of firepower."

"No." I sighed. "They can't."

"I've been collecting ships ever since we parted ways," Ashcroft said. "We've been fortunate in one respect. The Coriandon don't know about us. So we've got some surprise muscle on our side—but it's not enough. Not against two additional fleets. So here's the plan I have so far. The second wormhole is the closest." He indicated the display again. "We take our fleet, dash through this wormhole, and close it behind us. With the wormhole sealed shut, that denies the Coriandon an entire fleet. Against the other two, we might have a chance to defend Mars. Maybe."

"That's a big maybe," I said.

"The biggest."

"The real trick is how to seal the wormhole behind us," I said. "They don't exactly come with on-and-off switches."

The admiral leaned over the table and thumbed an intercom button.

"Send in Ensign Poppins please."

A woman entered the briefing room a second later. She was easily as young as Cindy, but that's where the resemblance ended. Bright red hair cut short like a boy's, slicked back and smooth. Skin a glaring white. Eyes the color of polar ice. Wide lips, pink. She wore a crisp uniform, brass buttons polished. Ensign insignia on her shoulders. Her perfect posture was as severe as the rest of her. She stood ramrod straight in front of the admiral, clicked her heels, and snapped off a salute.

"At ease, Ensign," the admiral said. "Tell Agent Sloan your idea for closing the wormhole."

"I was engineering track at the academy back on Mars." Each word flew out of her as precise as a scalpel cut. "I took a theoretical physics class and the professor postulated that a sufficiently large enough antimatter explosion could collapse a wormhole. It's never been tried, but the math is on his side."

"Define 'sufficiently large enough'," I said.

"Overloading a starship engine that runs on antimatter should do it," she said.

I looked at Ashcroft. "Do our ships run on antimatter?"

"No," Ashcroft said, "but the Coriandon ships do."

"I don't suppose you happen to have captured a Coriandon ship recently."

"We were hoping you'd capture one for us."

"This is a terrible idea," I said.

"Yes," Ashcroft agreed, "but it's the best terrible idea we've got."

THIRTY-ONE

As battle armor went it was pretty lightweight, meant to give me a chance against small-arms fire but still allow for maximum maneuverability. Utility belt with sidearm and extra magazines, grenades, and beamer. Exploding tips for the ammo, since they worked best against the gelatinous aliens. Sadly there was a limited supply.

We'd also each been given a laser cutlass, which had proved effective against the Coriandons at close range.

There would be two boarding parties. Since men and women with combat experience were in short supply, I'd been asked to lead one of the parties. A grizzled sergeant with a face carved from mahogany would lead the other one.

"I wish we had a company of fully augmented shock marines," Ashcroft had told me. "Wish in one hand and shit in the other. See which one fills up first. Am I right? So look, here's the best I could do. We need people on the team who can fly the ship once we capture it, but I want to make sure they've at least held a weapon since basic. I did the best I could. In a ship-to-ship battle, I'd put my people up against anyone else in the galaxy, but hand to hand? Well, they're not trained for it. That's why I need you."

"I'll take them in," I'd assured him. "Don't worry."

He would worry.

So now I stood in my quarters, trying not to sweat too much in the battle armor. Meredith helped me cinch the straps in the back and buckle the seals. In a pinch, the armor could double as a short-term pressure suit.

"Loosen up, okay?" She slapped me on the back. "If anyone can do this you can."

"Yeah."

She slapped my back again. Harder. "I'm serious."

I forced a laugh. "You said you were going to tell me about the metal disc on the side of your head."

"My attempt to be helpful," she said.

"Helpful to who?" I asked. "The Reich? I thought you weren't a fan."

"Well, I mean, it's different now, isn't it?" she said. "With aliens on our doorstep, humanity needs to stick together. Anyway, you'd be surprised how useless a spoiled heiress is on a battle hulk in the middle of a war. I don't want to be dead weight while the most important events in history are going on all around me. I had an implant, and now I'm downloading a lot of training. Takes hours, instead of weeks."

It was like she expected me to say something encouraging, or approving, but I couldn't quite manage it. All I could think of was Mueller telling me we were all becoming machines.

My door chimed. *Saved by the bell.*

"Come in."

Cindy started to enter, stopped short when she saw Meredith.

"Oh. I don't want to interrupt."

"You're not," Meredith said. "I was just about to leave." She started to move, and paused. Looked at Cindy, then back at me, then threw her arms around me, kissing me so hard she mashed my lips painfully against my teeth.

She pulled away and said, "Don't die, okay?" Then left without another word.

"I'm sorry," Cindy said again. "I thought you were alone."

"Stop being sorry. What can I do for you?"

"Just wanted to deliver the same message she did, I guess. About not dying. You already saved me once. I'd like you to live long enough for me to pay you back."

"I'd like that, too." And I wanted to gather her in my arms and kiss her hard and keep kissing her until the rest of the galaxy went away and it was just us. But then she'd be like any other girl I'd kissed, and I didn't want that because that would mean I was the same too, and the idea I couldn't be a better version of myself disgusted me. I didn't know what would happen, if I would come back in one piece. If I did, then I'd consider it all again, consider *her* again, and reconsider myself. "Come on. Walk with me."

We headed for the hangar bay. I was in a combat frame of mind and took long, determined strides, helmet under one arm, every muscle taut for action. Cindy almost had to jog to keep up.

We stopped at the door to the hangar bay, and I turned to her.

"This is as far as you go."

"Please come back," she said. She stood on tiptoe and kissed me on the cheek. I looked in her eyes for a long time, not even sure what I was searching for.

"I'll be back. I promise."

And then I boarded the shuttle with the rest of the doomed idiots.

"I'm going to go over the plan," Ensign Poppins told the boarding parties in the hold of the shuttle. "But first I want Sergeant Kolostomy to do a weapons check and brief you on any of the equipment you might not be familiar with. Sergeant?"

All eyes shifted to the mahogany-faced man with the crew flattop. The expression on his face said he'd just sucked a lemon full of broken glass. "You're probably wondering how you useless bags of crap are going to execute this bullshit plan and come out alive on the other side."

Poppins held up a finger, and Kolostomy shot eye daggers at her.

"Actually, Sergeant," Poppins said. "A number of the people here are junior officers, and technically your superiors."

The sergeant grinned, teeth like buttery piano keys. "Yes, ma'am. That's absolutely true, ma'am. If you like, we can review etiquette and practice saluting each other, instead of going over the information that might keep these people from getting ass-raped by giant wads of snot before being flushed out an airlock. Ma'am."

Poppins cleared her throat.

"I... uh... carry on, Sergeant."

Kolostomy glared back at the rest of us. "I am Master Sergeant Hamfast F. Kolostomy. The F stands for Fuck You."

He turned to the nearest trooper, an ensign who looked like he was twelve.

"What's that F stand for?" he asked, turning away.

"Fuck You, Sergeant."

Kolostomy wheeled on him. "What the fuck did you just say to me, you sassy-mouthed turd?"

The kid went pale. "But... you said..."

"Drop to the deck and give me a million," Kolostomy bellowed.

The kid went down and began doing pushups as fast as he could.

Kolostomy turned back to the rest of us. "In the last forty-eight years, I've fought eleven wars for the Reich. I've had every major organ replaced and have been shot and stabbed and burned with every weapon invented by people or aliens, so when I tell you that you're going to live through this, you had better by God believe me. Is that clear?"

The assembled troops muttered among themselves, as if trying to reach a consensus if the sergeant's claim was clear or not.

"I asked if that was clear, you maggots," Kolostomy bellowed.

"CLEAR, SERGEANT!"

"Here's the secret," Kolostomy said. "This is the nifty little trick that will keep you alive. You won't even have to write it down. It's so simple that even you brainless tenderfoot useless jackwads will be able to remember."

They all waited breathlessly.

I was curious myself.

"I hereby absolutely forbid you stupid dipshits to die," Kolostomy said, "and you dumb fuckers can consider that an *order*. The corpse of anyone who disobeys this order will be court-martialed, and I will *personally* come find your sorry asses in the afterlife, gouge out your eyes with my thumbs, and fuck the empty eye sockets. Is that what you want? To stagger around the afterlife blind and eye-fucked?"

No muttering this time—clearly nobody was eager for such a thing to happen.

"I asked if that's what you wanted," Kolostomy shouted.

"NO, SERGEANT!"

The kid doing the pushups had slowed considerably. Kolostomy kicked him in the ass. "Get the hell up. You can give me the rest later." To all of us he said, "Now how many of you have never worn this kind of armor before?"

Almost every hand went up.

"Son of a bitch, I've seen more intelligent kernels of corn in my shit. Listen up." He went on to explain the basics, stuff I already knew. The armor would stop most small-arms fire and a number of laser and other energy blasts before overloading. Still, it was a good idea to avoid getting shot at all. He went over the weapons, the exploding tips for the ammo, and the laser cutlasses.

"Just look sharp, and stay together," he concluded, sounding almost human now. "We all watch each other's backs and get our jobs done, we'll be just fine." He indicated Poppins with a nod. "All yours, Ensign."

"Thank you, Sergeant." Poppins fixed us with a hard stare, or at least she did her best. After the storm of Sergeant Kolostomy, Poppins's attempt at a tough expression just made her look gassy.

"This is the sector of space we're approaching now." She gestured at a 2-D monitor affixed to the bulkhead next to her. "There's a small moon next to a gas giant, and on that moon is a Coriandon supply routing station. In other words, supplies come from the home world to this moon, and are then diverted via freighter to wherever the supplies are needed. Our objective is to commandeer one of these freighters, and then overload the engine in order to collapse a wormhole. The admiral will be coordinating our run at the wormhole. For now, we're just focusing on getting the freighter."

A hand went up.

Poppins said, "Yes, Weinstein?"

"The Coriandon supply line will surely be guarded," Weinstein said. "I notice we have a zip ship along as an escort. Is that going to be enough to cover our assault?"

"The zip ship isn't along to provide cover,"

Poppins said. "We'll get to that in a minute. This entire operation depends on precise timing."

Poppins had already explained this to me, and I wasn't optimistic. I watched the faces of the others for reactions as she unveiled her scheme.

"The Coriandons have two battle fleets that they intend to send through two different wormholes to attack Mars. One of the wormholes is too far away for us to do a damn thing about it. But the closer wormhole, the one in this sector of space, well, that's a different story. They're sending almost every ship they have in this sector to that one." She made a big circular motion with one hand, indicating the area on the monitor.

"That means they're leaving only an undersized battle group in the territory behind them to respond to threats. The Coriandons are counting on a small handful of gunboats to patrol the entire area. They're spread thin. *Very* thin."

"They don't feel it's much of a risk," I said. "The admiral told me he's been fairly successful at playing hide-and-seek with the Coriandons. They don't even know we have a fleet in the area."

"He's right," Poppins said. "As far as the aliens know, all Reich fighting ships have withdrawn to defend Mars. That's one of the reasons we're moving so fast. At the moment we have surprise on our side, but who knows how long it will last."

"Not long, if the supply station radioes they're being attacked." This comment from the kid who'd been doing the pushups. "That'll bring the gunboats down on our heads pretty fast."

"And *that's* why we have a zip ship tagging along after us," Poppins said. "At the last second before our assault, the zip ship will put a couple of missiles into their communications relay buoy. Eventually they'll realize they're no longer getting a signal, but by then we'll have done our job."

She swiped the monitor screen, and the display became a schematic of a Coriandon cargo freighter. It wasn't what you'd call a pretty vessel. The whole thing was basically a box the length of a couple football fields, with an enormous engine attached to the rear end and a dome up front for the bridge.

"About thirty years ago, the Reich captured a Coriandon freighter that drifted across the line into our territory," Poppins said. "Intelligence suggests it's doubtful the design has changed much, since it's a simple ship for a simple purpose, and all of their innovation goes into their warships."

She tapped the screen, and the display zoomed in on a topside hatch located at the center of the ship.

"The shuttle will land over this hatch. We'll lock with it, and a small charge should be enough to blast our way in." She changed the display again to show us a wide corridor within the ship. "This is the main corridor that runs the entire length of the vessel. This is where our teams split. Sergeant Kolostomy's team will head forward to take the bridge. Agent Sloan will lead me and my team aft to the engine room, where I'll rig the engines to blow." She nodded to me. "Agent Sloan?"

"We're not expecting combat troops," I said. "If we're lucky, we might even catch them as they're rotating crews, so maybe there won't be so many on board. But I never count on luck, and combat troops or not, the bastards will find some weapons quickly enough once they realize they've been boarded. The plan is the same for the engine room boarding party as it is for the bridge boarding party. There is only one door in and out of each area. Seal the door and hold it. The blobby sons of bitches will only be able to get at you one at a time, and they'll lose enthusiasm after you scatter a few with exploding ammo." I turned to Kolostomy. "Sergeant, you have the most combat experience of anyone here. Anything to add?"

"You've got to move fast, fast, fast," he said. "Don't let the enemy get set. Don't give them time to react. You see one of the slimy bastards, you shoot. Don't wait to see if he's pushing a broom or loading a pulse rifle. Just shoot and keep shooting until the problem goes away. There's no prize for the trooper who comes back with the most ammunition."

"Sounds good to me," I said. "Ensign Poppins, it's your show. Any final words?"

"Do your jobs," she said. "Remember the plan. Stick to it, you'll be fine." She glanced at the computer screen. "Okay, we're almost there. One final equipment check while we've got the time."

As the teams began to check each other's gear, they murmured to one another. They were nervous. No—they were *afraid*, but checking the gear gave them something to focus on.

The crowed parted as Sergeant Kolostomy came through. He planted himself in front of me and tapped the portion of my helmet that covered my left ear.

"Just a heads-up. The universal translator is channel six, in case you want to talk to the snot wads."

"Is that something I'd want to do?"

"The hell if I know," Kolostomy said. "Just keep in mind the thing can't translate idioms for shit." He turned and went back to abusing his troops.

I had a feeling, palpable and real. It was the most sure I'd been about anything since being taken out of stasis back on Earth.

I was going to die.

Evidently I wasn't the only one feeling pessimistic. I spotted Poppins off alone in a corner, facing away from everyone else. I went to her. She was breathing in deeply, exhaling loudly. She did this over and over again, taking deep breaths and letting them out.

"Hey."

She turned to face me, eyes wide, knowing she'd been caught.

"I… I'm just…"

"Terrified," I said.

She hesitated, then said, "Yes."

"Everything you said was right. Everything Sergeant Kolostomy said was right. But none of it means this is going to work. You'd be insane not to be scared."

"I'm not sure if that makes me feel better or not," she said.

"Then don't feel better," I told her. "Where's it written you're allowed to feel better?"

"Nowhere, I guess."

"That's right. It's a shitty situation. If you didn't feel like shit when faced with a shitty situation, then that just makes you a dumbass. Not brave."

She swallowed hard, tried to smile, failed, then nodded.

"Now listen," I said. "It's just us talking now. I didn't want to say anything in front of the others, but you never said how we were going to get out once we'd completed the mission."

She shook her head, looked confused. "What?"

"Once we've set the engines to detonate," I said. "What's the plan to get back to the shuttle and escape?"

She shook her head, still confused. "Plan? There's no plan. We need to stay on board and make sure it blows at the exact moment. It's a one-way trip. The admiral didn't tell you?"

And then *I* felt like shit.

THIRTY-TWO

Two seconds after the zip ship had destroyed the communications buoy, we blew the topside maintenance hatch on the Coriandon freighter.

We dropped down into the ship's main thruway and landed in fighting crouches, guns up and ready to kill anything that looked like a green blob. Sergeant Kolostomy took his troops and sprinted for the bridge. Poppins and I took the remaining three troopers with us and headed aft. We didn't waste breath on *good lucks* or *goodbyes*. We all took Kolostomy's advice to heart.

Keep moving. *Fast*.

A Coriandon stepped out of a side corridor and didn't even have time to look surprised. One of the troopers next to me fired a burst of three, right into the globby bastard's midsection. There was a fraction of a delay before the explosive tips detonated. Green goo splattered in every direction and covered the walls and ceiling of the corridor.

A hatch opened, and another alien emerged to see what all the racket was about. The other two troopers peppered him with gunfire, and he exploded all over us. I wiped green glop off my face and kept running.

Still no alarms. We'd caught them flat-footed.

Although they didn't have feet.

Whatever.

We stormed the engine room. About ten of the aliens turned slowly to see what all the fuss was about. They blinked at us, still unaware their ship had been boarded, no idea who we could be or what we might be doing there, although in that split second when we all raised our weapons to fire, it may have occurred to them something had gone very, very wrong.

All five of us blazed away with our weapons, blobs screaming fear in their gurgle language and exploding, until finally there was nothing left but an ankle-deep layer of green slime. We moved in, weapons up in case one of them was hiding somewhere, all of us trying to keep our footing in the slippery goo.

"The engine controls are over here," Poppins said. "Cover me while I orient myself."

"Here's how we're going to do it," I told the troopers. "I want one of you down behind this control console to watch the door straight on. One of you find cover left, the other cover right. Any of the snot wads coming through that door gets a nice three-way crossfire, right in the face."

They saluted and took their positions.

I keyed the mic in my helmet.

"You there, Kolostomy?"

"We just secured the bridge," the sergeant's voice crackled in my ear.

"How fast can you get this ship in the air?" I asked.

"Fast."

"Do it. We don't want to give these jokers time to board any additional asset they might have hanging about."

"Roger that."

Two seconds later I felt a vibration through my boots. The ship shuddered, and we were away.

It had all been way too easy. Somewhere there was a gelatinous green sergeant cursing a blue streak at his green troops, and telling them how they were going to take their freighter back.

"How are we doing over there, Poppins?"

"Got it figured out," she said. "I can overload the engines, no problem. It's only the timing that's tricky. We need to blow them right as we're entering the wormhole."

I moved to stand right next to her, pitched my voice low so the troopers couldn't hear.

"So what about getting out of here, once you set the thing to blow." I wasn't going to die that easy.

Poppins shook her head. "It's no good, Sloan. We've got to hold the engine room, or the Coriandon engineers will just come in and dial back the overload. Then the whole trip is for nothing, and we're *all* screwed."

"I'm not saying we do anything to endanger the

mission," I replied, "but there must be a point of no return."

She frowned. "What do you mean?"

"The engines," I said. "Can they get so hot that the Coriandons can't back them down again?"

She thought about that for a second.

"Yeah..."

"Then there's got to be some time between the point of no return, and the actual explosion, right? It's a chance for us to get back to the shuttle."

"There's no way to accurately predict—"

"Fuck that," I said. "Come on, Poppins. You know your stuff. This is your show. I'll take your best guess any day of the week."

"It could be anything," she said. "Ninety seconds if we're lucky, but maybe five seconds."

"So let's get lucky."

She chewed her lip, thinking about it. She keyed her helmet mic.

"Sergeant Kolostomy?"

"Here, ma'am."

"I'm amending the plan," she said. "Listen up."

I caught the trooper looking back at us. It was the kid Kolostomy had made do the pushups.

"Eyes front, trooper," I said.

He snapped his head back around to watch the engine room doorway.

"Sorry, sir."

I eased up next to him. "What's your name?"

"Porkins, sir."

Poor bastard.

"We've got things covered back here, Porkins," I told him. "You just watch that door, okay?"

"Yes, sir."

"Stay cool. Things are going our way."

"Understood, sir."

I went back to Poppins. She was nodding, finishing up a conversation with Ashcroft. "Yes, sir. I'll let everyone know. Thank you, sir."

She turned to me, her expression grave. "The fleet is moving into position. They're going to drop out of translight as close to the wormhole as possible, and make a beeline for it. We form up behind them so we can go through last and blow the engines."

"What about the Coriandon fleet?"

"They're parked and waiting," Poppins said. "Ashcroft thinks that by the time they can respond, he'll already have his ships through the wormhole. Everything depends on speed and timing. I've already relayed the information to Kolostomy's team on the bridge. They're guiding us in. The only thing we need to worry about is timing the engine overload. We just need to sit tight until it's time."

That's when Porkins's head exploded.

My theory was that he'd taken his eyes off the door again. Otherwise he'd have seen them first, and could have started shooting. Not that it mattered now.

The other two troopers blazed away at the green mass coming through the door. Judging by the number of arms holding guns, there were at least three, maybe four melding together and all trying to ooze through the door at once. They fired pulse weapons into the room, hot orange blasts passing over our heads as we dove to the floor.

The exploding tips sent green goo splashing in every direction, squirting through the doorway like toothpaste, globs flying as the troopers fired on them. Part of the mass was growing arms and hands that grabbed the guns and fired into the room at us.

Fuck, that's just not fair, I thought.

I drew my pistol and fired along with the troopers, green gunk exploding and splattering over and over again. Suddenly the mass of green withdrew from the doorway like an emerald tide, washing back out to sea.

"They're withdrawing," I shouted. "Sound off. Who's hurt?"

"I'm good," Poppins said.

"Okay here." It was the trooper who'd taken up position on the right. The final trooper rushed to Porkins's side to check on him, but it was no good.

"Damn," she said. "Just... damn. Sergeant Kolostomy is gonna be pissed."

She looked young, freckled, like she might have been milking cows on the farm five minutes before they shoved her into a suit of battle armor.

"Hey, listen to me," I said.

She looked at me, eyes afraid.

"This isn't over," I said. "Take his place. Watch the door."

She hesitated, but only for a second. She swallowed hard, then nodded, and trained her pistol on the doorway and waited. She didn't look away.

"I've got the fleet," Poppins said suddenly.

"They're moving into the wormhole. I'm going to start overloading the engines now." She pressed some buttons and moved a lever forward until the hum of the engine grew more high pitched.

"Kolostomy!" she shouted into her comm. "Report."

"We're in line for the wormhole," he said. "ETA five minutes. We've got the Coriandon fleet on the scanner, but they haven't responded yet. Looks like clear sailing."

"Understood, Sergeant." To me Poppins said, "The engine's overloading now. If I've timed it right, we should hit the point of no return in four minutes."

The four longest minutes of my life.

A red light blinked on the control console next to Poppins. An ear-splitting alarm accompanied the blinking light, indicating the impending engine overload.

"That's the point of no return," she said anxiously. "If we're going, then now's the time."

I pointed to the trooper with the freckles.

"Check the hall. Now!"

She ran to the doorway, looked out, then back at me.

"Clear."

"Back to the shuttle," I shouted. "Run as fast as you can."

We sprinted from the engine room, hitting the main corridor and running back like bats out of hell. No Coriandons anywhere in sight—which struck me as strange. I keyed my helmet mic.

"Listen up, Sergeant. We've rigged the engine blow. Get your people back to the shuttle... *now*."

"It's no good, Sloan." The pop and rattle small-arms fire in the background almost drowned out Kolostomy's voice. "They're swarming us. Even if we could get past the sons of bitches, somebody's got to stay at the tiller and keep us on course. You people go. We've got this."

That explained the empty corridor. Most of them were assaulting the bridge. There was no time for plan B. No time for profound words.

"Good luck, Sergeant."

Halfway back to the shuttle they came at us, filling the corridor, shoulder to gelatinous shoulder, blocking our way like a wall of jello.

"Don't stop," I yelled. "Keep running as you shoot!" Pistols bucked in our hands as we ran and fired. The exploding tips obliterated the first line of Coriandon. We fired and fired until our pistols clicked empty.

No time to reload.

"Laser cutlasses!" I shouted.

I unclipped the hilt from my utility belt and thumbed the ignition button. The cutlass's red laser blade blazed to life and I waded into the line of green monsters, swinging with every ounce of strength I had. The glow blade made deep rents everywhere I slashed, the globby alien bodies slicing open like overripe fruit, and gunky alien guts spilling everywhere.

The others joined me on either side, Poppins on the right, the troopers on the left, swinging their own cutlasses, screaming battle rage, the rage of the desperate. I was covered in green slime, but I kept pushing forward, carving any alien that dared come within range.

"Cut a path!" I yelled.

We redoubled our efforts and the Coriandons fell back, high-pitched screams of panicked gurgle erupting with each thrust of my cutlass. Even with the urgency to escape driving me on, some part of me was just too curious. I switched my helmet to channel six for the universal translator.

"The blades of fire burn as do my Aunt Meelgra's feet."

"Oh, help us, mighty space turnip!"

Kolostomy had been right about the idioms.

"On me! Let's move, people. We have to push through *now*!" I charged for the weakest part of the line. We slashed and bellowed rage. I heard Freckles scream, and she went down under a quivering green pile. Just as Poppins and I broke through the aliens, the last trooper went down.

The words *"Turn his human flesh into brown soup!"* crackled though the translator.

I didn't want to know.

I shoved Poppins ahead of me.

"Go! Don't look back!"

We were up through the hatch fast. I sealed it on our end.

"How much longer?"

"I don't know." Poppins's voice was strained. "Any second."

We rushed forward, and I took the pilot's seat. Poppins strapped herself into the copilot's seat. I didn't think it possible for her to be any whiter, but she'd gone sickly pale. I guess I couldn't blame her. She was waiting for an antimatter explosion to go off under our asses any second.

I hit the thrusters, and the shuttle slowly pulled away ahead of the freighter.

Come on, you hunk of shit. Faster... faster!

I ordered the computer to remove all safety buffers and redlined the engines. The wormhole loomed large in the forward view screen.

The shuttle's engines roared and shuddered, the whole ship shaking. Warning lights flared bright across the control console.

"Bring up the rear view," I told Poppins.

She tapped at her keyboard, and a picture-in-picture display sprang up in the corner of the forward view screen, showing us the Coriandon freighter growing smaller behind us.

"The Coriandon fleet is responding," Poppins said, looking at the scanners.

"Can they get here in time to block us?"

"No."

"Then fuck 'em."

My eyes were locked on the freighter behind us. I realized I'd been holding my breath, forced myself to let it out. We'd enter the wormhole in seconds.

"Oh, no."

I frowned at Poppins. "What is it?"

"It's been too long," she said. "The freighter's engines should have overheated by now."

"Could the Coriandon engineers have reversed the overload somehow?"

"I don't know," she said. "I thought we were past the point of no return."

"But you don't know for sure."

"It's alien technology, okay? Damn it, I did my

best. This is why we should have stayed on board. We could have made sure."

She was right.

Damn her, she was right.

"Well, what the hell do we do now?"

"Shut up," I said. "I'm thinking."

We were upon the wormhole. No time to ponder. I grabbed the throttle, ready to turn the ship around. "We're going back."

"What?"

"If that fleet gets through the wormhole, we're screwed. We've got to go back and—"

The rear-view display flared blinding white. I shut my eyes and turned away. A split second later the shockwave hit us, slamming the ship, and throwing us against our restraining belts, carrying us along. The shuttle tumbled and threatened to rattle apart. Sparks danced across the console as systems overloaded. The displays winked out and the cockpit filled with smoke.

Poppins was screaming, but I could barely hear her over the blaring alarms and the groan of metal.

And then we were in the wormhole, swallowed by gray silence.

THIRTY-THREE

Poppins hung limp against her restraining straps. Blood dripped down one ear.

I coughed. A thick layer of smoke hung in the cockpit.

"Vent," I said.

Nothing happened. The computer was offline. Emergency systems kept the life support going, but for all intents and purposes we were dead in space.

At least we'd come through the wormhole.

Poppins stirred and groaned.

"Vent."

"I tried that already."

"Did we do it?" she asked. "Is the wormhole closed?"

"I don't know."

She tapped at the computer, trying to bring up the scanners.

"Everything's dead," I told her. "Almost everything. Shockwave hit us hard."

"I'm tapping into the reserve batteries," she said. "Give me a second."

I waited. A drink would have been nice.

Poppins sighed, flopped back into her chair, relieved laughter bubbling out of her.

"It's gone. The wormhole collapsed in on itself. It worked."

The radio crackled. Static then a voice.

"Shuttle, this is the *Pride of Nuremberg*. Anyone left alive over there?"

I laughed, too. "Nice to see you again, *Pride of Nuremberg*. If you can arrange a tow for us, we'd love to report to Admiral Ashcroft that we've just killed a wormhole."

They towed the bludgeoned shuttle to the battle hulk's hangar bay.

The gangplank went down and Poppins and I emerged into a roar of applause. Crew and officers from all over the ship had turned out to crowd the hangar bay and cheer our triumphant return. I took it all in with a grain of salt, remembering Kolostomy and the other troopers we'd left behind.

Poppins clearly had little experience of being the center of attention. Her smile was an odd mix of pleasure, irritation, and bashfulness. People patted us on the back, shouting "good job" and other pleasantries.

The crowd parted as the admiral headed straight for us. When he reached us he pumped Poppins's hand, then mine, grinning from ear to ear.

"You crafty son of a bitch, Sloan," he shouted over the din. "Part of me thought that plan didn't have a snowball's chance on Mercury, and I wouldn't have bet a single credit any of you would have made it back alive."

"More of us should have," I growled.

"Don't let it get to you," Ashcroft said. "You either, Poppins. Only so many miracles you can work. We'll mourn the dead later, and make the enemy pay for each and every one of them."

He leaned in close to talk into my ear. "You hurt? You need to see the doc or anything?"

"I'm okay," I said.

"Good. I need to see you in the briefing room in an hour. We'll let the crew have their feel-good moment for now. Good for morale, but the worst is yet to come."

"Yeah. I know," I said.

I had an hour. I showered, and was pretty sure I could spend the rest of my life in there. I stumbled out and got dressed—somebody had put a fresh laundered jumpsuit in my quarters. Fresh underwear. Fresh socks.

The door chimed.

"Come in."

The door slid open, and she rushed in, threw her arms around me and kissed me hard. She clung to me, desperate, the kiss going on so long I thought it was my new life. I put my arms around her and drew her close, feeling her slim body against mine.

* * *

Years later we pulled away from one another, breathless. She wiped tears from her eyes.

"They told me you weren't coming back," Cindy said. "They said you and the rest were sacrificing yourselves."

"We were supposed to," I said. "As usual, I fucked it up."

She laughed and sniffed and wiped away more tears.

"When you went away I… I don't know. I felt lost." She turned away. "I sound stupid."

I took her chin in my hand and turned her back toward me, her eyes huge and hopeful and filled with tears.

"It's not stupid," I said.

I kissed her, gently this time, my lips barely brushing hers, and I felt her tremble in my arms.

"It's not over, is it?" she asked.

"No."

"You might die tomorrow."

"We might all die," I said.

She looked up at me, a request so plain and basic in her face, I felt my knees go weak.

"I have to speak with the admiral."

"I know," she said. "Can I wait here?"

"Yes."

I kissed her again and left before I could say something to ruin it.

* * *

No 3-D display this time. We simply sat around the briefing table, and Admiral Ashcroft laid it on the line.

"If the other fleet arrives, we're pretty much fucked."

It was me and a few other senior officers. Poppins was there, too, looking like she might crap her pants at any moment. Still, her part in swiping the Coriandon freighter and collapsing the wormhole had earned her a seat at the adult table.

"We have Poppins and Sloan to thank for closing the wormhole and preventing those ships from joining the fray," Ashcroft continued, "but intelligence reports that the second fleet is much bigger than we anticipated. They're coming through the further wormhole, and if they arrive to join the Coriandon forces already bearing down on Mars, there's no scenario in which we can reasonably expect to be victorious. In short, we're seven hours from Mars, and the other Coriandon fleet is nine hours away."

"Two hours difference," I said. "That's a pretty narrow window for winning a war."

"I know," the admiral said, "but we've gotten word to our people on Mars, and they know we're coming. They're going to attack with everything they've got, and we're going to come in full steam from the other direction. We'll catch the Coriandon fuckheads in the middle. If we can win before the other fleet arrives, then they might figure it's not worth the effort, and turn back.

"It's our only shot."

There was muttering around the table, but finally everyone agreed.

"The plan is simple and straightforward," Ashcroft said, "and there's one thing that might tip things to our advantage." He nodded. "Go ahead, Poppins."

Poppins gestured toward the middle of the table, and a 3-D display blipped to life, rotating slowly so we could all see it from every angle. It was some kind of enormous spaceship—of Coriandon design by the look of it. The diagnostic information scrolling below it told me the ship was at least three times the size of the battle hulk.

"One of these will likely be leading the enemy fleet," Poppins said. "We call them class five ships, but roughly translated, the Coriandons call them..." She briefly consulted the notes on her tablet. "...the biggest turd in the bowl. Oh. That's not very nice."

"Fucking alien idioms," Ashcroft said. "Never mind, Poppins. Carry on."

"Coriandon ship captains aren't independent thinkers like Reich captains," Poppins said. "A single central commander—located aboard the class five ship—will almost certainly direct the entire attack. Eliminating the class five and the central commander should disrupt their strategies enough to make them withdraw."

"Can the battle hulk take on the class five?" I asked Ashcroft.

"No chance," the admiral said. "Even if we weren't completely banged up, toe-to-toe with a beast like that just isn't an option. I'll be leading the rest of the fleet against the other ships. It should be a fair match with the class five out of the way."

I could see where this was going.

"Why do I think getting the class five out of the way is the tricky part?" I said.

"Tricky, yes, but there's a way," Poppins said. "About a year ago, some of our operatives on New Bohemia got close to a class five and took some detailed readings. They also smuggled out some schematics. New Bohemia is right on the edge of Coriandon space, and they've been warning us for nearly a decade a Coriandon invasion was imminent."

"So did this detailed examination of the schematics reveal any weakness in the class five?" I said. Unless the answer was yes, we were screwed.

"It did," Poppins said. "The class five is so big and so well defended that the Coriandons don't consider a single, one-manned fighter to be a threat." Poppins gestured at the 3-D display again. It spun and rotated, zooming in on a round opening on the bottom of the hull nearly all the way aft. It was about forty feet wide and appeared to spiral open and closed, giving it a vaguely sphincter-like look.

"Examining the schematics indicates that Coriandon technology is highly advanced in almost every area except one," Poppins explained. "Plumbing."

I raised an eyebrow. "Plumbing?"

Poppins gestured again, drawing a line from the sphincter along the belly of the ship to the center. "A single zip ship can fly along this waste disposal tunnel, fire a timed torpedo at the central flushing station, and get out again before it detonates. The chain reaction will simultaneously back up every toilet on the class five. Our engineers are confident the vessel won't be able to stand up to that kind of stress. All the pipes will burst nearly at once and they'll be neck deep in their own yuck."

I frowned. Something about the plan didn't ring true, and anything that simple seemed doomed to failure. What sort of morons would fail to guard such an obvious weakness? Yet the more I thought about it, the more the idea grew on me.

Lends new meaning to "the shit hitting the fan," I mused.

She turned away, looking off at some imaginary faraway thing, a wistful expression on her face.

"Many Bohemians died to bring us this information."

"We've managed to scrounge up enough zip ships for a small squadron," Ashcroft said, "but we're critically short on pilots. What we really need is somebody with a cool head and iron in his spine to make the torpedo run."

All eyes in the room turned to me.

Oh, just fuck you, people.

THIRTY-FOUR

I walked slowly back to my quarters, lost in thought. Ashcroft had suggested that I get some sleep. I didn't see how that was possible.

Still, I was tired. So very tired. Since I'd been awakened and taken out of the cryo-chamber, I'd teetered on the brink of one crisis only to tumble into the next and the next and the next. The notion of a long, peaceful sleep seemed like the most pleasant thing in the galaxy.

Until I entered my quarters, and Meredith was waiting for me.

"From the look on your face, I guess they told you," Meredith said.

"You know the plan?"

She tapped the metal disk on the side of her head. "I told you I'd been taking accelerated training. Guess

I should have mentioned it was for piloting a zip ship."

"You're going?"

She nodded.

"You might want to reconsider," I said. "Chances are good we're not going to make it back from this one."

"We know," said a voice from the corner.

Cindy stepped into view, nervously nibbling her bottom lip.

"We've had a little talk," Meredith said.

Shit.

"You have my attention."

"We're grown-up modern people, and we know tomorrow might be the end for all of us." Meredith moved closer, put a soft hand on the side of my face. "It's a stupid time to be competing. It's a time to share, don't you think?" *Oh…* I thought.

Cindy moved closer, too, put a shy hand on my chest.

"This is okay with you?" I asked her.

Her eyes were both frightened and excited. She nodded quickly, like she didn't want to give herself a chance to change her mind.

I bent and kissed her gently as Meredith's hand unzipped my jumpsuit and reached inside. I returned the favor, unzipping her, my other hand pulling Cindy close, the gentle kiss becoming more earnest as our tongues connected. I turned and kissed Meredith.

Cindy tore at her own clothing, anxious to get undressed, and that spurred Meredith and me into action, too, all of us shimmying out of jumpsuits and kicking away underwear.

Fuck sleep.

The three of us tumbled to the bed, clinging to one another. Meredith scooted back against the wall, sitting up and spreading her legs. She pulled Cindy back against her so that her head rested on Meredith's breasts. Meredith cradled the girl, offering her to me, and I remembered that while she might have had the appearance of a twenty-two-year-old woman, Meredith was mature, and definitely confident. She didn't need to be first—not in this case.

On the other hand Cindy was shy, and needed to be guided, which Meredith was more than willing to do. She cupped Cindy's small breasts, petting gently.

Cindy looked up at me, mouth open, breathing shallow, face flushed. "Please." The word leaked out of her barely above a whisper.

"Please."

I positioned myself over her, but she didn't want to wait, grabbing me and guiding me in. She bucked her hips, desperately, like she'd been waiting for this all of her life. Meredith held onto her. Cindy arched her back, mouth open, working silently, eyes shut tight.

I leaned down and kissed Meredith over Cindy's shoulder.

I picked up speed, and Cindy reached around me, latching on, trying to pull me deeper inside of her. The three of us fell into the same rhythm, and moments later Cindy trembled beneath me, the sound of a lost, forlorn animal rising out of her.

An hour later, I had no trouble sleeping at all.

THIRTY-FIVE

The zip ship squadron had to be in position well ahead of time, so the six of us were parked for over an hour in the shadowed crater of a large asteroid. With the engines off, we didn't expect to emit an energy signature large enough to be detected. We were nervous anyway. The Coriandon fleet was scheduled to pass right over us.

I looked right and left out of my cockpit's bubble window. I knew Meredith was parked on my starboard side, but with the running lights off I could only just make out the outline of the vessel in the darkness. I would like to have talked to her, but we were maintaining radio silence.

The stars glittered brightly, space stretching endlessly, vast and silent. That there wasn't enough room for all the species seemed suddenly ludicrous.

I monitored the feed coming in from the Reich fleet. When the battle started, I'd be able to follow the action. In the meantime, there was nothing to do but wait for my opportunity to fly straight up the asshole of an alien spaceship, so I could torpedo their toilets.

Another hour stretched by.

We felt the Coriandon fleet before I saw it. Vibrations came up through the asteroid and my seat in the zip ship. The vibrations became a rumble, rattling my teeth, and the first Coriandon battleship passed overhead, a massive juggernaut filling the view, another right behind, and more alongside. Not counting the little fighters flitting between the big ships, there were at least a hundred vessels in the fleet. Poppins had been right on target in her prediction of where they would drop out of translight.

The fleet passed, the rumble fading, and then silence descended again. A minute passed.

Two minutes.

Five.

I let out a sigh of relief. Poppins had been wrong. The class five wasn't the anchor ship of the invading fleet. The other five zip ships and I could rejoin the fight. We'd have a chance.

Then the rumbling started again, growing louder and more acute than the sounds of all the previous ships combined. The zip ship shifted beneath me, and I worried for a panicked second the asteroid was crumbling to pieces.

Then I saw it.

It blotted out the stars. Seeing a 3-D schematic of the class five in no way prepared me for the reality. It seemed as if it took *weeks* for the ship to pass over us, a massive planet-demolishing behemoth. The looming effect stemmed in part from the fact that it was traveling at a much slower speed than the ships which preceded it. This was what Poppins had said about the Coriandon strategy. The class five would hang back, directing their forces and only engaging if it were necessary.

This worked to our advantage. The rest of the fleet would be far ahead. Turning back to assist the class five would take time, and by then our work would be done.

We hoped.

The class five finally passed, and the stars returned. The spaceship lumbered away like some lethargic beast, heedless of the insignificant flies that buzzed around it.

I waited two more minutes. Then I took a mini-light from my belt and flashed it out of my cockpit bubble, first starboard and then port. The adjacent ships relayed the signal to the others. A moment later we all fired engines. I lifted off first, and the other zip ships fell into formation behind me.

We took off after the class five.

A moment later, the fleet feed squawked with the first report. Missiles rose from the surface of Mars, streaking toward the enemy. The alien ships maneuvered into a perfect defensive formation, and picked off each missile as it came. They'd been prepared for just such an attack and retaliated with textbook precision.

Which left them wide open to the unexpected attack from Ashcroft's fleet. As the first of their ships exploded in brilliant fireballs, the Coriandons scrambled to reconfigure, and that's when a battle group rose from the planet's surface. Reich ships slammed into the Coriandon fleet from two directions. The ships moved into point blank range and pounded each other mercilessly. The damage on both sides was staggering.

But that wasn't my problem.

The class five hove into view—we'd almost caught up. An alarm beeped, drawing my attention to the sensor screen. A dozen lamprey ships—named for the fact that they clung to the bottom of larger vessels until sent into battle—dripped from the bottom of the class five's hull and spun to meet us.

"Incoming lampreys," I said over the radio. No point in maintaining silence. "They're bigger and much less maneuverable than a zip ship, but they're armored like a motherfucker and armed up the ass. You've got to juke and jive. Do that, and you have a chance."

We only had a few seconds.

"I'm making a run for the class five. You've got to keep them off me." I didn't say what everyone already knew. The zip ships only had one way to keep the lampreys occupied, and that was to fly around and let themselves get shot at.

"Meredith, stay with me. I want you helping me gun a path all the way in."

"Roger that, Sloan."

The next second we were among them. Meredith and I broke one way, the remaining zip ships rolling in the other direction. One of the ships took a pulse blast immediately, and disintegrated into fiery dust. The rest scattered without discipline, the lampreys chasing in groups of twos and threes.

I had my own troubles. A lamprey made a beeline directly for us from the front, trusting to its armor. Instead of breaking away and taking evasive action, I ordered Meredith to hold steady. If I'd ever doubted her courage, I didn't now. Hot orange blasts from the lamprey's pulse cannons flashed over, under, and in-between us as we sped down the fucker's throat.

"On my mark, concentrate fire on the cooling coil below the lamprey's cockpit," I said.

"Just hurry," Meredith said.

"Now!"

We both fired together. The coil glowed hot and exploded, taking the rest of the lamprey with it. We sped through the debris field, nothing now between us and the class five.

"We lost another zip ship," Meredith's voice squawked in my earpiece. "They're catching hell back there."

"Can't be helped," I said. "Stay focused." We were close enough for me to see the big sphincter in the lower aft section of the Coriandon vessel. "Come on, Poppins," I muttered to myself. "You've been right so far. Be right now."

I kept flying. Kept waiting.

"Shit." Meredith's voice.

"What is it?"

"Two of the lampreys have broken off," she said.

Fuck.

"Stay with me," I said.

"That's not going to work," she said.

"Meredith."

"Somebody's got to keep them off of you, and you know it."

She was right. Damn it all, she was right.

"I'll see you on the other side," I told her.

"Bet your sweet ass." She hit the brakes, spinning the zip ship around, and pushed full-thrust back toward the lampreys.

Eyes forward. I hit full thrust for the sphincter.

Come on, you giant asshole. Come on.

And then it spiraled open.

"Yeah! That's what I'm talking about," I bellowed. "Poppins, you gorgeous pale ghost!"

The reports had indicated that the sphincter opened and closed on a regimented schedule, sure as magnesium. According to Poppins, once the class five entered the fray, it would make sure to jettison any extra mass.

Including sewage.

I flew toward the sphincter at full speed just as a wall of milk-brown crap came blasting out. The cockpit bubble went all over brown, the shit-storm buffeting the zip ship so fiercely I was afraid I'd lose control. I'd suddenly become the galaxy's unluckiest salmon, swimming up the worst imaginable stream. My arms ached trying to hold the ship on course.

Abruptly it stopped, and I hit the running lights. I was through the sludge, hauling ass down the class five's rectum. One thing was an absolute certainty. If I made it through this alive, they were going to have to wash this zip ship for days.

Right on time, I neared the central flushing station,

hovering there as I lined up the shot. It was a bulky metallic thing like some ancient boiler, hundreds of pipes feeding in and out of it from every direction. I put it in my crosshairs and fired.

The torpedo pierced the huge boiler, goo spurting back out the hole. The impact started the countdown, and the mechanism started to buckle on every side, metal bending and twisting and shredding. Every pipe and conduit connected to it ruptured and exploded. I spun the ship and hit full thrust back down the tunnel, and after what seemed like far too long, I was in open space again.

A second after that two lampreys were on me. There was no sign of any other zip ships. I banked hard just as a volley of pulse blasts flashed past me. Maneuvering the zip ship in tight near the class five, I skimmed the surface of the hull, figuring the lampreys wouldn't risk firing and hitting their own ship.

I figured wrong.

They snugged up right behind me, blazing away. A pulse blast caught one of my foils, and I almost wrenched my shoulder out of my socket trying to keep the ship from smashing into the class five's hull.

One of the lampreys behind me exploded.

What the fuck...?

"That's one," Meredith's voice crackled in my ear. "Bank left and you'll lead the other one right in front of my guns."

I whooped joy and banked left. When we got back to the *Pride of Nuremberg*, I was going to show my gratitude in new and unusual ways.

The second lamprey exploded, and I pulled away

from the class five, Meredith joining up on my wing.

"Lady, I can't even tell you how glad I am to see you."

"Sweet talker."

"Where are the other lampreys?"

"We took them out," she said.

"And the other zip ships?"

A pause. "Just me."

"Let's put some distance between us and that class five," I said, trying not to think about it. "That torpedo's going to blow soon."

We took up a position about five miles out and watched. The countdown clicked off on my heads-up display.

"Three...

"Two...

"One!"

Nothing.

Shit! I hated when things didn't explode like they were supposed to.

"What now?" she asked.

"Just wait," I told her. "Sometimes these things don't happen on cue."

Five minutes later it still hadn't happened. No *ka-boom*.

"Oh, no." Her voice sounded tired, defeated. "You've got to be fucking kidding me."

"What is it?"

"Check your sensors," she said. "The class five is launching more fighters."

I checked the sensors. Then double-checked. She was right. Dozens more. No, *hundreds.*

I was cursing up a storm when she started laughing. The poor woman had cracked up.

"They're not fighters," she said. "They're escape pods. Fucking escape pods!"

I checked the sensors again. The Coriandons were abandoning ship. The class five began venting in several places, the enormous vessel listing awkwardly and drifting away. It amused the hell out of me to imagine its corridors filled with alien shit. And the smell...

I decided not to think about it. Not so amusing after all.

Meredith and I turned our zip ships toward Mars to join the battle, but a few minutes later we got the word from Ashcroft. All Coriandon ships were withdrawing. They were turning tail to run.

We'd won.

THE FINAL CHAPTER

The battle hulk had taken a flabbergasting amount of damage, but miraculously it had survived.

Again.

We parked the zip ships in the hangar bay and an officer told me I was immediately wanted on the bridge.

"The admiral wants me," I told Meredith. "Back as soon as I can."

She threw her arms around my neck, kissed me hard. "I'll be waiting."

Armed with that incentive, I double-timed it to the bridge, passing repair teams and medics carrying wounded to the sick bay. The crew was tired, but not defeated. There was a stubborn pride in them, something that straightened their postures, brightened their eyes.

We'd won. Against all odds, we'd done it.

When I stepped onto the bridge, Ashcroft came toward me, grinning like a madman. He shook my hand and clasped my shoulder. The first mate and Poppins both stood at their stations, smiling approval.

"Agent Sloan, you crafty son of a bitch!" he said. "Is there anything you can't do?"

"Thank Poppins, Admiral," I said. "It was her plan."

Poppins nodded respect in my direction.

"They're going crazy on the surface," Ashcroft said. "It's like a festival down there, people partying in the streets. The chancellor seems to be missing at the moment, but as soon as he can take the podium, he's going to address the entire planet. It's already being called one of the greatest victories in Reich history."

Admiral Ashcroft could barely contain himself. He was practically giddy. He'd come through it all, taken everything the aliens had thrown at him, and given back double. I wouldn't be surprised to see him drunk soon with the rest of the revelers. He'd earned it.

We all had.

The door opened behind me, and I smiled wide as Cindy stepped onto the bridge.

My smile wavered as I took a look at her.

She wore a black uniform, brass buttons in a bib formation, the swastika with the dragon perched on it over her heart. Her hair was back in a long braid down her back, eyes darkly lined, black lipstick, grin odd and deranged. She didn't emit the subliminal power of the clones, but she was no longer the demure girl I'd known a few hours ago either.

I tried to process what I was seeing. To understand the obscure joke.

"What's all this then?" Ashcroft said.

Cindy lifted a small automatic pistol and squeezed the trigger. The bridge shook with the blast, and the back of the admiral's head exploded, brains and blood and skull splattering out. He fell to the deck, the metal half of his face clanking hard.

The first mate opened her mouth to scream, but Poppins was there with another pistol and blew a hole in the side of her head. She fell, trailing blood, landing in a tangled awkward heap.

For the first time ever, none of my training kicked in. I didn't move to attack or to defend. I just gawked. Something jabbed my side, and a jolt burned through every part of my body. Suddenly I was on my hands and knees, trying to clear my head.

A stun wand. Someone had hit me with a fucking *stun wand*.

More people were coming onto the bridge, stepping around or over me to take up positions at the various stations. My head swam, but I was conscious enough to look up and see Poppins standing in front of Cindy, snapping off a crisp salute.

"Bridge secure, ma'am," Poppins said.

"Excellent," Cindy said. "Are we ready to broadcast?"

"Soon," Poppins assured her. "Our people on the ground are already spreading the word that their new chancellor will address them."

"Bring up the planetary news feeds, and put them on the big screen," Cindy said.

The big screen flickered to life with a scene from the capital city down on Mars. Hundreds of thousands of citizens crowded the main square in front of Gestapo headquarters. A group of men and women unfurled a huge red banner from the roof, and it hung down between the building's fluted columns. It proudly displayed the swastika, the brass dragon perched on top, wings spread grandly. They erected a thirty-foot-high view screen next to the banner.

Suddenly Cindy was kneeling next to me, a smug gleam in her eye.

"So easy. I knew from your profile you wouldn't be able to resist the demure girl who so needed to be saved. So shy. So vulnerable… and you. So predictable. If you had a row of buttons across your forehead, they couldn't be any easier to press. You so desperately needed to see me a certain way, didn't you? Because then you could think of yourself differently. You're flesh and blood, Sloan, but you might as well be a robot for all your programming."

I wanted to tell her to go fuck herself, but I was fighting the effects of the stun wand. Dizzy. Darkness coming and going.

"I am the daughter of the Brass Dragon," she said, "and I've come to claim my birthright."

"Ma'am, we're ready to broadcast," Poppins said.

Cindy stood and turned away.

"Put me on."

Her face suddenly appeared on the thirty-foot screen in the square, the crowd hushed, turning to her. My eyes went blurry, but I blinked them clear. I needed to see this.

"Citizens," she said, her voice ringing across the square. "I am Cinder Josephine Cleopatra Heintz, the direct descendant of Joseph Heintz, the Brass Dragon, and your new chancellor. I have arrived to deliver you from the Godless alien invaders and to lead the Reich into a glorious new future."

The crowd cheered wildly. Just like that Cindy was the new chancellor, the ruler of Mars and whatever was left of the Reich Empire. I mean, it had to be true, right? I'd just seen it on TV.

And then I passed out.

I awoke in the brig and stayed there awhile, alone. A couple of hours went by. The daughter of the Brass Dragon was the new supreme ruler of the Reich Empire, and I helped put her there.

Agent dumbass.

My cell door opened and two burly men entered, each holding a stun wand.

"Get up."

"Time for the firing squad?" I asked.

"Sooner or later I guess," one of the guards said. "First, a little interrogation. If you know anything useful, we need to squeeze it out of you, maybe have some fun in the process."

"I suppose this involves a fresh cup of coffee and some earnest conversation," I said.

"It involves electrodes on your gonads."

Damn.

A hand cracked one of the guards in the neck. I heard a sharp snap, and he went down.

Meredith moved into the room, arms up in perfect fighting posture. The second guard swung the stun wand and she blocked it, her other hand shooting out, the heel of her palm slamming the guy's nose flat. It exploded blood down the front of his uniform, and he staggered back.

She pressed forward, spinning in a roundhouse kick that connected to the side of his head and put him down.

I gaped. "What the fuck, lady!"

"I've been downloading martial arts training for a week," Meredith said. "Come on!" She took my hand and dragged me out of the brig.

We came to a crossroads, and she looked both ways down the wide corridors of the battle hulk. Nobody around.

"The passcodes on my yacht are still the same," she said. "Most of the crew is celebrating the victory, so you should be able to sneak to the hangar bay, no problem."

"Me? You're not coming?"

"Everything's confused right now, but you can hide out on one of the frontier planets and come back to join me later," Meredith said. "I'm useful here. I'm part of this. I can't leave."

"But it's fake," I said. "All a lie."

Her face fell, and I saw that my words genuinely confused and saddened her.

"How can you say that? We defeated the aliens. We *saved* the Reich."

"You *hate* the Reich."

"That was before," Meredith said. "Don't you see

that everything's changed? We're *humans,* and we've got to stick together. When I was spoiled millionaire Meredith Capulet back on Luna, I thought I could give my life meaning by buying it. Like it was some kind of hobby. It's different now. I laid it on the line and came through the other side to tell about it. I can't give that up. I can't let that be meaningless. I'm needed here, and I've never been needed before."

The weight of unreality was suddenly too much for me. How could I explain about the clones and Mueller and all the lies that had brought us where we were now?

I couldn't. The truth would crush her. I wouldn't be the one to take away everything she thought she had.

"You're right," I said. "You stay here where you can do some good."

She brightened and kissed me. I let the kiss linger an extra moment, knowing it would be the last.

"Okay, get out of here," she said. "While you still can." Then she turned and trotted back down the corridor.

On the way I met some drunken members of the crew. They toasted the victory. Toasted the Brass Dragon. One stopped me in the hall and gave me a high five.

"Hey, you're the agent guy that flew the zip ship into the big toilet right?"

"Sort of, yeah."

"Nice job, man!" Fist bump.

I'd almost made it to the hangar bay when I ran into a trio of crewmen, arms around each other, beers in hand. They toasted me, slurring words.

"Yo, man. You know the five-oh-first fight song? That's our fucking outfit."

"Sorry," I said. "I'm not very musical."

They passed me and began to sing, loud and off key. "Hey hey, we're the Nazis... and people say we Nazi around!" That gave me incentive to keep moving, and fast.

I found the hangar bay and let myself into Meredith's yacht. I strapped myself into the pilot's seat and calmly initiated the startup procedure.

The hangar bay doors were closed.

I donned the headset, adjusted the mic. "Hangar bay control, I need the doors open and clearance for takeoff."

A second later, a drunken voice crackled in my headset.

"Hey, where you... *hic*... where you, uh, going?"

"Beer run," I said. "We're dangerously low. I'm also bringing back a half dozen of those android prostitutes with the pheromones."

"Oh, shit yeah. Yeah, that's... *hic*... that's cool. Can you, like, get a bag of Curry Crisps while you're out?"

"Affirmative."

A second later the hangar bay doors slid open.

I eased the yacht out and turned away from the fleet. Meredith had told me to head for the frontier, maybe a little green rural planet where the Reich would forget about me, and then, at some future time, we'd meet up again. But I knew it would never happen.

I left the bright garish red of Mars behind me, and turned the ship toward the darkened Earth.

EPILOGUE

The bodies were still there. The agency cryo facility had been long abandoned. What did a few bodies matter? It seemed a lifetime ago that the man in the glitter tie had arrived to bring me out of stasis.

I stepped over him, wiped the dust off the cryo computer and prepped the chamber. There was usually a lab tech for this, but I knew the routine. I stripped down and lowered myself into the chamber, closed the door to my glass coffin.

Eventually, I would be plunged into total oblivion, a frozen darkness as brain functions slowed to almost nothing, but it was a slow descent, and I dreamed at first.

Meredith and me, and Cindy was there too, all of us tangled together so completely that we might have been one. Cindy's face hovered in front of me, lips black, smile predatory like an animal's. Her face elongated, fangs growing from her mouth until I was looking at a dragon, scales a gleaming brass.

The dragon spread its wings and took flight, soaring past the clouds and into space. It sped between stars and grew enormous, a beast unrivaled.

It breathed a fire that consumed the galaxy.

AKNOWLEDGEMENTS

Thanks as always to my agent David Hale Smith. Thanks to my editor, Steve Saffel, and to the team at Titan Books, including Nick Landau, Vivian Cheung, Laura Price, Miranda Jewess, Paul Gill, Julia Lloyd, Chris Teather, and Hayley Shepherd.

And thanks to my family, who love me for some reason. Most of all, thank YOU, readers, who seem to get me. Lunatics like us have to stick together.

ABOUT THE AUTHOR

Victor Gischler lives in Baton Rouge, Louisiana with his wife and son. He can usually be found next to his charcoal grill. His novels include *Gun Monkeys, Go-Go Girls of the Apocalypse*, and the fantasy trilogy *A Fire Beneath the Skin*. His comic book work includes runs on *Punisher MAX*, *Deadpool*, *X-Men, The Shadow,* and *Angel & Faith*, and his creator-owned book *Sally of the Wasteland* was published by Titan Comics. He is the winner of Italy's Black Corsair award for adventure fiction. Gischler is a world traveler and amateur beer-swiller.

COMING SOON FROM TITAN BOOKS

MARCH OF WAR

BENNETT R. COLES

The Centauri terrorist was stopped, but not before he caused widespread death and destruction on Earth. This leads to an escalating war. Lieutenant Jack Mallory is on the front lines, leading a flight of Hawks into the battle zone. His mission is to rescue Thomas Kane, whose Astral forces are under fire.

The Astral Force must establish a bridgehead in Centauri territory, where they will place a jump gate in anticipation of a new invasion. Lieutenant Katja Emmes works behind the scenes, to keep the Centauri from learning of the plan before it can be carried out successfully.

AVAILABLE 2017

TITAN BOOKS